STILL WATERS

COMPASS BOYS, BOOK 3

JAYNE RYLON

MARI CARR

HAPPY ENDINGS PUBLISHING

Copyright © 2018 by Jayne Rylon

All rights reserved.

No part of this book may be reproduced or shared in any form or by any electronic or mechanical means—including email, file-sharing groups, and peer-to-peer programs—without written permission from the author, except for the use of brief quotations in a book review.

If you have purchased a copy of this ebook, thank you. I greatly appreciate knowing you would never illegally share your copy of this book. This is the polite way of me saying don't be a thieving asshole, please and thank you!

If you're reading this book and did not purchase it, or it was not purchased for your use only, then please purchase your own copy. Refer to the don't-be-a-thieving-asshole section above for clarification. :)

Cover Art By Jayne Rylon

Editing by Mackeznie Walton

Version 2

eBook ISBN: 978-1-941785-88-1

Print ISBN: 978-1-941785-89-8

Compass Boys, Book 3

A brand new, never before released standalone story in the Compass saga from New York Times and USA Today bestselling authors Jayne Rylon and Mari Carr.

Bryant is unlike other relentlessly alpha Compton men, including the three cousins he loves like brothers. While they grew up drooling over pretty girls in Compton Pass, he was sneaking peeks of the sexy men working his family's ranch.

All that sweaty, shirtless skin... flexing, exposed muscle... tight, dusty jeans... The temptation proved too much. As a reckless teen, Bryant let a cowboy kiss him in the barn—a decision with horrifying consequences.

Grateful for college and a chance to escape the aftermath of his mistake, Bryant buried himself in his hydrology studies. Missing his family while he learned how to tame his cowboy craving seemed like fair punishment.

Now, with his education one thesis project away from completion, Bryant still isn't prepared. There's a gorgeous cowboy tattoo artist not-so-patiently waiting for him to return from academic exile.

Vaughn's gracious offer of assistance on Bryant's water conservation experiment at Compass Ranch is simultaneously a relief and the ultimate torture. One final test Bryant may just flunk. Because Vaughn is determined to cannonball into the deep, still waters of Bryant's repressed sexuality.

Content warning: Contains a brief but graphic depiction of a sexual assault.

PROLOGUE

Bryant Compton held his breath. Was today going to be the day he finally found out what it was like to kiss a cowboy? Or any guy, for that matter?

He prayed it was.

"Like what you see?" Vaughn Sevan looked up from arranging gear in the barn's tack room and flashed him a wicked grin that emphasized his dimples. They peeked from beneath sooty scruff that speckled his strong jawline. The deep shadow there enhanced the ultra-white gleam of his wolfish smile. His Armenian roots were showing. Damn, they were sexy.

Bryant tried to say yes. Instead, all he could manage was a gulp. He swiped his dusty forearm across his parched lips, wondering why he hadn't brought a bigger water bottle with him that morning when reporting to the barn for chores.

Snake's son had only recently started working on Compass Ranch after coming to live with his ailing dad, who'd had Vaughn late in life after a not-so-wise hook-up with a woman he'd met at a wild rodeo after-party out of state. Two years older than Bryant, Vaughn had crossed his path on summer breaks and other visits in the past. However, it was only since he'd become a permanent fixture at the ranch, taking over Snake's duties while caring for his father, that he'd begun strutting around with his shirt off, sweat rolling down his tanned back, and his powerful legs visible through the rips in his jeans. That's when Bryant realized just how gorgeous and cut the other guy was.

Vaughn chuckled, then leaned in to whisper, "What do you plan to do about it, big guy?"

"Uh." Bryant choked. Sure, he was taller than Vaughn by a couple of inches, but he'd bet he was a hell of a lot less experienced. At least if Vaughn's assessing gaze had anything to say about it. You know, that and the fact that everything Bryant had ever done with a guy had taken place in his fantasies.

What the hell could he do? While the ranch was overrun with alpha males, there weren't many role models for the kind of relationship he thought he might like to have. Was he supposed to take charge? He'd much rather let Vaughn have the reins.

Except his hesitation spoiled the moment.

Vaughn backed up a step, his smile dimming some as he angled for the door. "Ah, shit. I forgot. Despite your grown-ass body, you're still just a kid."

"Hey, I'm almost eighteen. Going to college out of state in a couple of months on a full scholarship." That didn't sound juvenile to Bryant. So what if he hadn't technically accepted yet? Or even broken the news to his parents, for that matter.

It didn't impress Vaughn much, in any case. He took another step back, his boot heels clunking on the wide old floorboards as he jammed his hands into his pockets. "I heard you were smart. Maybe you should start acting like it instead of teasing losers like me in your daddy's barn—somebody might take you up on it. You're not ready."

I am. I mean, I'm pretty sure I am. Bryant tried to ignore the sting of rejection that needled him more and more with every bit of distance his crush put between them. Maybe that was why he made one of the dumbest decisions in his life next.

He watched Vaughn spin around and disappear into the yard, and heaved a sigh of regret. Why had he frozen at the last second? If he'd gone for it, swooped in and taken what he'd wanted, maybe they'd be making out right now. He could have tucked himself against Vaughn's washboard abs and defined chest, wrapped his arms around Vaughn's trim waist and held on tight. Instead, he'd let Vaughn see that he was unsure of himself and...well, now he was standing here alone.

Or at least he thought he was.

"Hey, don't worry about that asshole," someone—he thought it might be the guy who'd just signed on this week—said as he came out of the shadows behind Bryant, scaring the ever-loving shit out of him. Damn it, whoever it was had overheard his whole mortifying swing and miss. "What does he have to be so damn arrogant about? He's, what, a whole year older than you?"

Ignoring the flaming in his cheeks, Bryant tried to gauge whether the hand who'd obviously witnessed his failed flirtation was about to bash him for being gay.

Around Compass Ranch, testosterone flowed like the river in the gorge after a spring thaw. He'd listened to his cousins endlessly lusting after girls. It made it tough to be himself sometimes. Not that anyone had intentionally given him shit, he just didn't have anyone who could really relate.

This guy was new. Who knew what he'd put up with...

"If you want someone to show you the ropes, why not go with somebody who's been where you are? I'd be happy to teach you a thing or two." The cowboy nudged Bryant until they swung fully into the tack room, lost in a dark cranny of the barn.

A stranger? A much older, harder man. Without the vibrancy and youth of Snake's son.

But he was here. Vaughn wasn't, and didn't seem like he was interested in taking the guy's place anytime soon. Bryant just wanted a kiss. A taste of what his cousins had already experienced.

Hell, Austin had made out with Clover Willis in the woods behind school in the sixth grade, and he and James were fooling around with their homecoming dates before the king and queen had even been crowned earlier that spring. Even Doug, his youngest cousin, had made it to second base by now.

Bryant just wanted one damn kiss. To know, for sure, that it was what he craved.

"That's right, don't let anyone tell you what you can and can't have," the guy coached as he approached.

He held perfectly still as the ranch hand knocked Bryant's hat from his head then leaned in, trapping him against a weathered post. His heart pounded in his chest. He should probably listen to the sliver of his brain telling him this wasn't the right way to do this. That this guy didn't know anything about him, didn't care about him, was at least twice his age.

He was being used…

To be honest, the majority of his seventeen-year-old brain didn't give a damn.

He just wanted to know, once and for all, if it was as good as he imagined it might be.

Bryant moaned softly when the guy kept coming. "Hey, uh, could you at least tell me your name first?"

"Bill. Make sure you scream it later." He lowered his head and crushed his mouth against Bryant's.

Bryant was still wondering exactly how a kiss would make him scream. Especially because it wasn't exactly how he'd pictured it, but he couldn't deny that his cock reacted to the pressure of the guy's sloppy tongue.

He parted his mouth, struggling to take a breath. Bill didn't stop there. He deepened his hold, making Bryant wince when teeth bruised his lips from both the inside and outside. He'd been decked before. Had laughed and wiped away the blood from a split lip one of his cousins had given him when they'd argued about something unimportant. But he hadn't expected to be hurt right then, by a guy who seemed to be into him. He'd thought it would be more...pleasurable.

Bill jammed his dirty hand down the front of Bryant's jeans and growled, "You like that, don't you?"

"I guess," he attempted to say. His timid response was devoured by the ranch hand, who seemed to be getting off on what they were doing. Maybe Bryant was the weird one for not enjoying it as much as he'd anticipated.

He scrunched his eyes closed, trying desperately to magnify the warm, tingly feelings and suppress the warning bells, which leaned toward panic or even pain. When the man fisted Bryant's cock in his hand and squeezed, Bryant couldn't help his reaction. He instinctually rocked his hips toward the tight grip, fucking dry into the man's calloused fingers. It might have been rough, but his body still responded. In fact, if he wasn't careful, the guy would end up with come all over his hand.

At seventeen, it didn't take much to set Bryant off.

"See. You're into it. Don't act like you're not. We don't have time for coy."

He was right about that. It wouldn't be more than twenty minutes until the rest of the hands came in from the far pastures, where they'd been mending fences before they sent Bryant and this guy back to get the stalls ready for the rest of the work horses.

"Okay, sorry." Bryant swallowed hard. No one's first foray into intimacy was perfect right?

If he passed up this opportunity, who knew when there would be another?

None of the other guys around the ranch—or in town, for that matter—would look at him twice. Compass Ranch was home to some people in unconventional relationships, including his uncle Silas and uncle Colby, who were both married to his aunt Lucy. There still weren't any openly gay Comptons, though. Besides, everyone knew it wasn't good for your long-term employment options to fool around with the boss's kid. Since their ranch paid well and had better benefits than nearly all other operations in a three-state radius, they tended to attract the best of the best. Which apparently also meant something about morals and shit.

Once Bill realized who Bryant was, he wouldn't be offering to jack him off anymore either.

"Can I touch you, too?"

"Hell yeah." The man unbuckled his pants and shoved his jeans to his knees. He wasn't wearing any underwear, something that surprised Bryant, though he couldn't say why. The guy's dick was hard if sort of disappointing. It wasn't anything like the ones in the porn he'd snuck a peek at on his laptop. "What? Ain't you never seen a cock before, boy?"

Bryant shook his head. "I mean, not other than mine or my cousins', but that's not the same."

"No, I don't suppose it is." Bill grinned, revealing a few missing teeth and several others that needed to be pulled. "In that case, come take a closer look." He crumpled the front of Bryant's shirt in his fist and yanked, sending Bryant sprawling on the floor.

He caught his balance, keeping himself kneeling at least even if he might have a chip in his kneecap.

Bill stepped closer, putting his cock right at eye-level. Or mouth-level.

It wasn't any more impressive from this vantage point. The guy had obviously been sweating out on the job, but Bryant licked his lips anyway. He'd always wondered...

Bill laughed as he speared his fingers into Bryant's hair and used the grip to position Bryant's mouth near his cock and balls. "Get it in your mouth. Suck it, like you want to."

Bryant did want to. Sort of. But he also was having some pretty serious doubts. What if Vaughn came back? He scanned the interior of the barn. Nobody was around.

Who was he kidding? Vaughn had made himself perfectly clear. He wasn't coming back.

Bryant swallowed hard, then thought of how Vaughn had dismissed him because of his inexperience. Maybe next time he wouldn't be so eager to walk away. Maybe if Bryant knew what he was doing, he'd have a shot at seducing the guy he really wanted...

He closed his eyes and pictured Vaughn, the predatory flash he'd had in his eyes the day he'd stumbled upon Bryant and his cousins skinny dipping in the back pond a few weeks ago. What if he'd been alone? What if he knew how to handle a guy like Vaughn?

It was time to learn so that he'd be prepared for next time.

Bryant parted his lips. The cowboy did the rest. Bill wrapped his hand around the nape of Bryant's neck before tugging him toward his crotch. It felt so weird when the guy's dick slid along his lips. Slippery and salty when it plunged into his mouth. At least it wasn't huge, so he didn't choke or anything. He'd hardly gotten used to the heat and weight against his tongue when the guy began to rock his hips, fucking Bryant's face with coarse shoves and grunts.

He figured that meant he was doing something right, so he tried sucking on it some.

It wasn't horrible. In fact, by now he was pretty damn hard.

So he reached down and cupped his aching shaft and balls.

Bill noticed. "You were made for this. Do it much more and I'm going to ruin your fun before we get started."

Started? With what? They'd already done more than Bryant had dared to imagine.

He pulled back to clarify, "I thought... Maybe I could get you off and you could do the same for me. Like this."

"Nah, we're not stopping here." The man shook his head. "You don't know what you're missing out on. Let me show you."

Vaughn had been right. Bryant wasn't ready for that. For more.

"I don't think—"

Bill gripped his upper arm and flung him around. It was right about then Bryant realized he'd been overconfident in himself and the protection afforded by his family's name. Hell, this guy might not have even realized Bryant was a Compton, son of one of Compass Ranch's owners.

His gut hit the corner of a bale of hay, knocking some of the wind from him. "Hey, I'm not sure..."

"Oh no. You're not going to back out now, are you?" Bill sneered as he shuffled between Bryant's knees. "You led me on. You can't get me hard and ready to fuck then leave me hanging."

"Sorry, I didn't mean to. I never did this before." Bryant shook his head, trying to think clearly. Had he given the guy the wrong impression? Yeah, probably. But that didn't mean he couldn't change his mind, did it?

What was the right thing to do?

While he debated, Bill didn't hesitate. He yanked Bryant's jeans to his knees, then shoved between his shoulders, hard. His chest smashed into the hay. And next thing he knew, the guy was mounting him, shoving his cock through Bryant's crack, nudging his asshole as he growled.

"Don't you need...?" Bryant swallowed his objection, embarrassed to even say the word *lube*. That probably should have been a clue to himself that he wasn't mature enough for what was about to happen.

Instead, Bill spit on his hand, then rubbed it around a bit before holding his cock down with two fingers and spearing Bryant with it. Thank God it wasn't even half as long or thick as Bryant's own dick. It hurt bad enough as it was.

Bryant roared, then bucked, trying to dislodge the guy. Unfortunately, Bill dealt with unruly horses for a living. Bryant didn't stand a chance.

"Stay still. Give it a second. You're going to love this." Bill didn't waste any time. He began riding Bryant, slamming into him hard enough that his balls slapped against Bryant's taint. Bryant was half-excited and half-terrified. Neither eclipsed his pain.

He gave it a second.

He still wasn't having fun.

Bryant shouted, "Enough! Get off me! I changed my mind."

"I'm almost done." The guy huffed, then slapped Bryant's ass, hard. "Stay still. Man up and take it. Fuck yeah."

"No, stop!" Bryant started to panic. He balled his fists but couldn't reach around far enough to get in a swing at the guy taking advantage of him. "I'm serious. Stop. *Please...*"

Just as he was about to freak the fuck out, someone shouted, "What the hell is going on in here?"

In that moment, Bryant felt relief first, followed immediately by a sickening wave of humiliation and shame.

Jake.

Bryant couldn't see what happened then, but he felt Bill's cock being ripped from his body around the time he heard a dull thud that sounded like a fist smashing into someone's face. *Oh shit. Oh shit.*

He scrambled to his feet, yanking up his pants as fast as he could given the shock of his body and the utter disappointment mixed in with the rest of the swirling emotions assaulting him. Something he'd dreamed about forever had just gotten utterly wrecked. He'd learned his lesson.

Cowboys weren't for him.

"Get the fuck off this ranch. You're fired. And if I ever see you again, you'll lose more than your job over this," Jake snarled, enraged and dangerous in a way Bryant hadn't fully realized he was capable of. He was seeing a lot of the world for the first time today.

"Who gives you the right?" Bill had the bad sense to argue. "You're just some old man—"

"He's part of our family," Bryant barked. It was one thing for someone to come at him, but no one messed with Jake. He stood beside the man he'd come to think of as a surrogate grandfather.

"None of the Compass brothers will stand for you attacking innocents around here, least of all one of their own children." Jake spit at the man. "Go ahead and try them if you think they'll be more lenient than me. You'll find I'm a cuddly teddy bear in comparison. Start with Silas. He's always had a soft spot for Bryant. This kid might even be Si's favorite nephew. It'll be fun to watch how you handle yourself with someone your own size. Your own age. Someone far stronger and faster, too."

Bill paled. The consequences of what he'd done were finally beginning to sink in. "I didn't need this piece-of-shit job anyway."

"That's good. Because once I spread the word about how you're compensating for that tiny cock by abusing young men, you're not going to get another offer within a thousand miles of here." Jake crossed his arms and spread his feet wide. "Get out of my sight before I change my mind about kicking your ass on the way out."

Without another word, the guy turned and ran, his belt buckle clanking with every step. He hadn't even bothered to finish getting dressed.

Bryant sagged against the tack room beam. Thank god the barn was there to hold him up.

His family, the ranch—they would always be there for him to lean on.

Even when he'd been a colossal idiot.

"Are you hurt bad, kid?" Jake winced as he caught sight of a streak of blood on Bryant's pants. It wasn't anything life-threatening. Alarming enough to make them both realize what might have happened if Jake hadn't sensed something was off and come to check on him, though. Had Vaughn tipped Jake off somehow?

Bryant dusted off his jeans and forced himself to stand straight. "I'm fine."

"You're not. But you will be," Jake promised.

"I just wanted a kiss," Bryant croaked. "That's it. I swear."

"You're a handsome kid, polite, charming, and you've got more brains than everyone else on this ranch put together. There's somebody out there for you. Somebody who will respect you."

Bryant studied the wood grain in the floor intensely. "I don't know. It's just...the Compass Curse, you know? No one will even look at me once they figure out I'm a Compton." He shrugged one shoulder. "Every eligible guy in this damn town stays half a mile away from me because they're afraid of my dad and uncles. And you, of course."

"Well, the smart ones are anyway." Jake grinned. "Didn't mean to cock block you."

Bryant groaned and tried to erase that phrase and Jake using it from his memory. In fact, he wished he could delete the entire day from his medial temporal lobe. He hoped they could walk out of here and never mention it again.

"Jake, please. Don't tell my parents, okay?" He swallowed hard, trying his best not to disgrace himself further by crying. But when he thought about having to admit what had happened to his father or Uncle Silas...shit. The last time he'd done that he'd probably been five and had gashed his arm bad enough to need stitches when he'd ignored Jake's advice not to chase his cousins with pitchforks in this very same barn.

Damn this place.

He thought of the letter he'd gotten yesterday, the one he hadn't even told his family about yet despite bragging to Vaughn about it.

His mind was instantly made up. He *was* going to go away to college.

"Kid, I don't know..." Jake slapped his hat against his thigh. "That bastard should go to jail for what he did to you. Your uncle Sawyer would have him locked up in a second. You know that, don't you?"

Bryant nodded. He did. And that was the problem.

"I don't feel right about that." Bryant cleared his throat. "I might have led him on. I wanted to see what it was like and... well, now I know."

"You don't know shit, Bryant." Jake whipped a glare in his direction. "If you think that what happened here today is anything like it should be when you make love with someone you care about, and who cares about you, you're nowhere near as genius as I thought you were. Hell, even if you were just looking to hook up and have a little fun...nope. That's not what I saw and *heard* as I came into this barn."

Bryant's face burned. He stared at his boots.

Then things got even worse. Vaughn bolted through the door. News traveled fast in a small town, faster still on the ranch. "Son of a bitch, Bryant. Are you okay?"

"Fine." Like he would admit anything else to the handsome young cowboy who'd turned him down flat.

"Vaughn, time to get back to work." Jake came to the rescue again. "I've got this covered. Thank you for your concern."

Though he opened his mouth as if to argue, Vaughn closed it. They both knew he needed his job to support Snake, who was going downhill fast. "Yes, sir. Sorry."

"No need to apologize. Just go on now."

With a final lingering glance over his shoulder, he nodded and left.

Jake mumbled, "Boy, he's the one you should have been screwing around with."

"I tried. He isn't into me." Bryant might as well admit it. He had no pride left to object.

"Hmm." Jake made a sound somewhere in between disbelief and wisdom. Had it been some other day he almost certainly would have had more to say about the matter than that simple harrumph. But both of them were a little talked out.

They'd shared enough for one day.

If only Bryant had stayed and listened, he might have saved himself a whole lot of pain and longing. Because for years after, no one could measure up to the beautiful boy he'd lost before he'd ever had him.

1

SIX YEARS LATER

Bryant spun around lazily on a swivel-top stool. He sat at the one of the tall tables in his college's hydrology laboratory. He couldn't believe he was running out of time here. The science complex had become his haven over the past six years. It was never really home, exactly. More like a sanctuary.

Even though he'd been in academic exile, he'd stayed away knowing someday he'd take everything he learned and apply it, improving his family's ranching operation back in Wyoming. Still... For a while, it had been a safe place. One where he was judged by his performance and his own actions exclusively, independent from the expectations or privileges that came along with the Compton name.

After years of taking extra credit loads and advanced coursework, he was set to break the record for the fastest time to earn a PhD in water conservation engineering from his college. All that stood between him and his diploma was one final project. To be exact, it was the proof-of-concept portion of his dissertation, which had otherwise been complete for nearly a month. The theoretical work had all been approved by the school board. Now he had to show that what he'd hypothesized on paper could work in reality.

The science of it all didn't scare him. Equations were made to be solved. And he was damn good at it. The emotional impact of returning home—not for a quick holiday visit, but to stay—well, that was kind of freaking him out. He didn't want to lose the self-sufficient person he'd discovered he could be at school in the herd of Comptons waiting for him to rejoin them. Plus, he felt like he might have been so busy sticking his head in his books that he wasted his chance to stick more fun parts of himself in more fun places. Once he went home, the opportunity to explore his sexuality as a relative unknown would be gone for good. And lately, he'd found himself thinking about relationships more and more.

It must have been because his cousins Austin and James had recently become infatuated with two particular women, reminding him of what he'd been missing all this time.

Only one person would understand why. Jake.

Okay, maybe two, but he would never talk to the other about his anxieties. It was better if he forgot Vaughn Sevan existed. Otherwise he'd start showing up in Bryant's dreams for a do-over of that fateful day as he sometimes did. As much as Bryant tried not to think about the sexy cowboy, it was hard not to when Jake constantly updated him about the guy. Even his sister, Sterling, periodically mentioned that Vaughn had asked how he was doing when the two of them got together for their coffee breaks at their neighboring shops in town.

It was hard enough to pretend Vaughn, and the terrible event he was linked to in Bryant's memory, didn't exist from here. How the hell would he manage it at home?

Bryant reread the long line of scribbles covering his whiteboard. He wished it was as easy to solve the rest of his problems. Whether or not he was ready, he was going to have to face them soon.

As if he were psychic, Jake chose right then to call.

Bryant grinned as he connected his phone for voice only. Unlike Bryant's cousins, the Compass Boys, the gruff old ranch hand hadn't embraced the video chat functions the rest of the world now considered default. "Hey."

"How's it going, kid? Haven't heard from you in a while. That usually means something's up."

"Here I thought you had super powers. I was just thinking about you." Bryant couldn't wait to share his thoughts about what he could do for the ranch.

Although he'd earned a free ride to university, his parents had still sacrificed by letting him go. It took enormous amounts of manpower to run Compass Ranch. A young, strong guy could be a lot of help. Over Christmas break he'd realized Jake had slowed down. Hopefully he could start picking up some of the slack.

"If I could have a super power, I wouldn't waste it on knowing when you wanted to talk to me. I'd fly. Or have laser-beam eyes. No...time travel. That's it. There are a few things I'd like to change about my younger, foolish days." Jake sighed then.

"Me too." Bryant echoed his sentiment, though he could only imagine how much more Jake had suffered, especially over the loss of the love of his life. Haiwee had left him about a half a century ago, taking Viho—their unborn son—with her. She'd passed away before Jake could reconcile with her. On top of that, he'd spent decades completely oblivious that Viho even existed.

Maybe it was time Bryant bucked up. Things could be so much worse than his petty drama. Letting one bad choice ruin the prime of his life might be even stupider than the original mistake he'd made.

After a slightly awkward pause, Jake said, "I was just calling to check up on you. What was on your mind? I'm guessing you wanted to chat about more than the weather. That's usually Doug's specialty."

Bryant could imagine Jake kicked back in one of the wooden chairs on the porch of the main house. Probably with a toothpick between his lips as he fished the remnants of Aunt Leah's lunch from between his charmingly crooked teeth. She cooked for him and the rest of the hands most days.

"Yeah." No sense in denying it. "I have to finish some practical application stuff for my final project. I think it could be really useful for Compass Ranch. Kill two birds with one assignment, you know?"

"That doesn't sound like a problem," Jake said.

"It's not going to be cheap." Bryant sighed. "The grant I applied for was denied since I've already hit the lifetime max for student financial aid through my scholarship."

"What's this project do? And don't tell me in your fancy scientist mumbo jumbo either." Jake snorted.

Bryant thought of the holistic system he wanted to implement in layman's terms. "It's a top-to-bottom water conservation, capture, storage, and delivery system. Think of it as drought-proofing the ranch."

"For the livestock or the crops?" Jake clarified.

Although Compass Ranch focused on cattle, there were a bunch of side shoots of business that had developed over the years. Uncle Seth bred horses, and they'd started growing extra hay to sell in case of rough times. Austin had even expanded his trucking services to haul stuff for their neighbors.

Diversification removed some of the risk from ranching. None of it could function without water. Bryant hoped to protect them all from a crisis situation by ensuring they always had a sustainable hydrological plan, especially given the impact of climate change on the region.

"Both." He started to get amped up. "Given the high evapotranspiration rate of the current straw variety, we could start with switching to more tolerant species, then use soil additives and plant border landscaping to retain more moisture. I've designed proprietary fixtures and an irrigation delivery network to manage outlays on as small as a plant-by-plant basis. I'd also fortify the drinking supply for the cattle by building a collection system that feeds an underground storage network, a few dams, and retaining ponds. Then we could focus on the purification of wastewater, recycling it instead of letting it run off. With all of the improvements taken into account, I estimate we could supply the ranch with at least two cycles worth of water to be rationed during droughts. That is, once the system comes up to maximum capacity."

"What did I tell you about that fancy shit?" Jake growled. "I think what you're saying is that you know a way to guarantee the ranch could keep on as usual even if it didn't rain for two whole years?"

"Yep." Bryant nodded even though the other guy couldn't see him. "Probably more. Because if we can also revamp the consumption side—"

"Bryant, that's enough." Jake cut him off.

He wasn't excited to hear the rest? Damn, maybe Bryant had misjudged the ranch's needs.

"I mean, you don't have to pitch me any more than that. That's worth a hell of a lot, kid." Jake chuckled. "Your dad can be tight with the ranch's purse strings, especially with all of this season's expenses, but if you can show him a solid plan to do what you just said, he'll be writing you a check so fast his pen will melt."

"A six-figure check? Seriously?" Bryant should have figured Jake would understand his hesitation.

This was the first time he could prove to his family that his education had been worthwhile. That what he'd done while he was away had the power to make an impact at least as big as Austin's with his truck-driving, and James's with his life-saving jumping-out-of-planes manliness, and Doug chasing those tornadoes.

Sometimes brains were just as important as brawn, right?

He sure hoped so.

"Yeah, of course." Jake got quieter then. "I'm proud of you, Bryant. They are, too. If you can pull off even half of what you think you can, you'll be making a big difference around here. Fuck, it's only April and it's fifteen degrees above average. Mark my words, by July we're going to be scorched. We'll need some help to make it through this year. The sooner you can get home, the better."

Bryant didn't know about that. The sooner he went home, the sooner he had to deal with the consequences of his bad decisions. Hopefully he'd be far too busy to worry about the ghosts in the barn.

Hey, it had worked for the past six years. Why not a few more?

Whipping out his super powers again, Jake must have picked up on his silence.

"Have you been letting loose any out there?" Jake wondered, his casual tone one Bryant knew was anything but innocent.

"Nope." He had a clean conscience there. "I've been studying and working my ass off. It hasn't been easy to finish these three degrees in the time it takes most people to earn two."

"Hmmm." Jake could show a lot of disapproval with a single sound. Sort of like he had that day...

"What *hmmmm*?" Bryant was wiser now. He asked and Jake let him have it.

"There are plenty of things to learn besides stuff you read about in a book."

"Like what?"

"Like how to find a boyfriend, for one. What to do with him

for another." Jake sounded like he'd gotten to his feet and was pacing the porch.

"I promise, I learned my lesson, Jake. I'm not going to fool around with the cowboys, causing a ruckus for you, my dad or uncles, or anyone else back home by screwing the help. I swear."

Jake cursed beneath his breath. "You idiot, that was never the problem. *You* weren't the problem."

"Then my choice to wait for the right person—someone I care for, someone I trust—shouldn't cause any issues either." It felt good to say it out loud. When his cousins teased him about his living the monk life, he brushed it off. With Jake, he could be honest. The guy knew why he felt that way.

He didn't have to explain or relive those terrible moments. Jake got it.

"If that's how you really feel, you're right. There's nothing wrong with that." Jake paused then added, "But if you're avoiding intimacy because you're afraid to open up again, well...*that* doesn't sound healthy."

Fear and denial caused Bryant to lash out. The instant he opened his mouth, he wished he could call his words back, but they were gone and said before he could stop them. "Is that why you never found another partner after Haiwee?"

Jake grunted as if her name was like a punch to the gut. His breathing was ragged for a few seconds, ones Bryant felt insanely guilty about.

"I'm sorry, Jake. I shouldn't have said that."

"You're entitled to call me on my bullshit. Someone ought to have years ago." The old man sounded even older now. "Don't be dumb like me. Be smart, like you. Okay?"

Bryant chuckled since Jake was wiser than most people he'd ever met. "I'll do my best."

"Maybe you should consider discussing this with Colby when you get home," Jake suggested. "Or maybe even Vaughn."

Bryant pointedly ignored the V-word.

"Uncle Colby? Why?" He was incredibly likeable, charismatic, and easy to talk to, but Bryant couldn't see where the guy would have any input on his sex life that could be helpful. Plus...his uncle? No thanks.

"He'll understand where you're coming from. Clayton, too. Either would be a good choice if you need someone to vent to." Jake was confusing Bryant more and more.

What would one of his cousin Hope's two husbands have to say about gay hookups? Wait... "You mean because they both have lovers that work the ranch, right? I told you, you don't have to worry about that."

"Bryant, you have got to be the most emotionally dense kid I have ever met."

"Then enlighten me."

"You know that Silas and Colby are as in love with each other as Clayton and Wyatt are, right? They're not only in the relationship to share their woman. They share each other, too. It's a three-way connection."

At that, Bryant spun himself a little too hard. His stool tipped precariously, nearly dumping him on his ass on the linoleum floor. He gaped at his phone before wheezing, "I mean...I guess. Sort of. I never really thought about it that explicitly. But choosing ménage isn't the same thing as being gay."

To him it seemed kind of normal. He'd grown up with Uncles Silas and Colby and Aunt Lucy, who loved each other as much as they loved their kids and nieces and nephews. Besides, Uncle Silas was mean enough to pulverize anyone who dared object or upset his partners. Bryant was pretty much his polar opposite.

"Nah, you're right. It's probably more common. Downright boring." Jake laughed. "Yep, kid. You're not as freaky as you think. Nowhere near as freaky as your mom, for example. Back in their day, your mom and dad and I and about a half dozen other cowboys used to—"

"No. Nope. Stop right there. I am not interested in hearing what you are about to say."

Jake laughed harder until he fell into a coughing fit.

"You okay?" Bryant asked when he didn't recover right away.

"Haven't felt quite right lately. Must be getting a cold or something. I'll be fine." Jake brushed off his concern, then hammered home his point. "Look, we want you home and we want you happy. Take some time to think about what I've said and we'll discuss it more when you get here, okay?"

Bryant tried to believe Jake. "Okay."

"Quit worrying. Everything's going to be fine."

"Thanks, Jake. I miss you." Bryant slumped on his stool. Maybe he could do this after all. With a little help from his mentor.

"You know I'm only a phone call away. And soon I'll be bugging you every day in person." Jake chuckled. "You'll be sick of me in a week."

"Never."

2

———

As it turned out, Jake had lied to Bryant for the first and last time in his life.

Everything was definitely *not* fine. And Bryant would never get another chance to talk with his surrogate grandfather, no matter how desperately he needed to.

Jake was gone. Dead.

He'd had a massive stroke in the very same barn where he'd saved Bryant and spent so much of his life.

Bryant still couldn't believe it was real. He rolled up to the red light at the center of Compton Pass, Wyoming. It looked mostly the same. A row of cute shops—including his sister Sterling's handmade-jewelry boutique—a diner, the police and fire stations, a couple of bars for the cowboys, and a sign pointing toward the hospital just outside of town. But it didn't feel the same. How could it?

He'd gotten the call less than seven hours ago.

Within five minutes, he'd dropped everything, packed some essentials, and left his college existence behind. Forgotten. When it came down to it, this town and his life here were most important.

Except a huge chunk of that was gone. Jake.

Just like that. The only good thing about the situation was that Jake hadn't suffered a long illness like his grandparents. At least that's what his cousin Austin and his girl, Hayden—who'd stumbled across Jake moments before his death—had promised Bryant when they'd called him home.

There was no way he was ready to turn onto the ranch's gravel driveway knowing Jake wasn't there and never would be again. It felt wrong, like it would if the barns were demolished or the cattle vanished or his family moved and didn't bother to tell him.

Bryant swerved into a parking spot in front of the retail strip. Maybe he'd stop and talk to Sterling first. She'd texted him that she had to finish a custom order before she could head over to the ranch. He could catch his breath and steel himself for going home, a place that was forever changed.

He remembered when his grandmother had passed away, but he'd only been a kid. Now he understood the significance of what they'd all lost. Including his brother-in-law, Viho, who was Jake's son. Oh God, it only got worse the more he thought about it. Had Jake known how much he meant to them all? What an integral part of Compass Ranch he'd been?

Bryant hoped so because now that he wanted to tell him, he couldn't.

He slid out of his truck, bracing his hands on his knees when the world wobbled a bit. He'd driven straight through, his mind racing faster than the miles that had passed beneath his tires. He wasn't Austin, a road warrior, used to long-haul trucking. Eating anything had been out of the question. For a nerd, it was a lot to handle.

"Hey, Bryant? Is that you?" a concerned person asked. "Are you all right?"

For a second, he flashed back to that awful day in the barn. Then he realized why. Although he hadn't heard it in more than half a decade, and despite it being deeper and gruffer than he remembered, he recognized the voice.

Not now. Not here.

Bryant had known it was inevitable. He couldn't keep avoiding the guy once he became a resident of Compton Pass again, but he absolutely wasn't prepared to deal with a reunion today, when he was already raw and damn near at his lowest.

"Vaughn?" Bryant straightened a little too fast, smacking his head on his side mirror in the process. "Ow! Shit. Yes. I'm fine. Or I was. Damn it. What are you doing here?"

Of all the people in Compton Pass—okay, so there weren't *that* many people in the town—he had to stumble across this one the instant he returned? What had he done to royally piss off the universe?

"That's my tattoo parlor. I was cleaning up, getting ready for this evening's hours, and saw you pull in. For a second I thought maybe you'd come to see me until I realized you're probably looking for Sterling." Vaughn cleared his throat. "Anyway, I wanted to tell you how sorry I am."

Bryant squinted at him. "Sorry?"

His brain scrambled, trying to clear their awful shared history from his mind and focus on this atrocious day instead. Surely Vaughn wasn't talking about way back then. Was he?

Bryant rubbed the spot he'd smacked. Maybe he'd hit it harder than he thought...

"About Jake." Vaughn kicked the curb with the toe of his boot. "I know you two were close."

Ah, shit. Bryant wanted nothing more than to run away. But where would he run to? Home? No, that's what he'd been running from in the first place. Stuck between Vaughn and the thought of going to Compass Ranch without Jake to greet him, Bryant propped himself against his truck, relying on it to hold him up.

Besides, he was being selfish. It would be impossible to miss the pinched set of Vaughn's sexy mouth or the heaviness in his gaze. "You worked for him a long time, too. Everyone's going to miss that old bastard."

Vaughn chuckled. "Yeah, that's true. He was there for me after my dad died. And… Well, yeah. He helped me through a lot of shit in his own tough-love way."

At any other time, Bryant would have asked what he meant by that. Right then, he didn't have the energy to take on anything but standing upright and making it through the next second.

"I hope you know I'm here if you need anything," Vaughn said gently.

Bryant hated the pity in his stare, and yet, he wanted nothing more than to lean on the one guy he should have resented. The one who'd pushed him away before. That was fucked up. But it didn't make it any less true. He subconsciously angled toward Vaughn, who reached out to steady him with a firm grip on his upper arm. Vaughn's thumb brushed up and down in a slow arc.

The simple, comforting touch seared Bryant as if it had been one of the ranch's branding irons instead of Vaughn's hand on skin. He was pretty sure he'd be able to feel the imprint of Vaughn's fingers forever after.

Bryant swallowed and resisted the urge to make a fool of himself with Vaughn. Again.

Before he could figure out what to do or say next, his sister saved him.

"Bryant!" Sterling shouted as she flew out her shop door and sprinted toward them. "You're home."

When she neared, she flung herself into his arms, forcing him to be strong for her and reminding him that he'd need to be there for the rest of the family, too. He caught her and hugged her hard enough that she squeaked.

Vaughn gave them a look that was tough to read. Envy? Regret? Disdain?

Bryant couldn't tell. But the guy started backing up again, just like he had that day years ago in the barn. Fuck him. Bryant wasn't going to let Vaughn's judgment affect him. Not again. And he certainly wasn't going to start making bad decisions just because the man was the sexiest person alive and Bryant craved his approval.

He was *far* too intelligent for that. And he had the 4.0 GPA to prove it.

If he could find solace with his family, that was his best bet.

"See you guys at the services," Vaughn mumbled as he turned and ambled back to his tattoo shop.

"Vaughn, wait!" Sterling called out, stopping him. "My mom said there's going to be a bonfire tonight. Informal. You know how it is. Everyone's dropping by anyway and the casseroles are stacking up. You're welcome to come. Eat. Share stories. Get through this together."

She flicked her gaze between Vaughn and Bryant. Could she sense the tension in the air?

"I'm sure he's busy," Bryant snapped before pointing at a handwritten sign lettered in a badass script that looked a lot like his cousin Austin's tattoos. Ones Vaughn had done. He was a hell of an artist. Bryant would give him that. He was even better than his dad had been, and Bryant had often admired his own father's and uncles' massive back tattoos, courtesy of Snake. "The shop is open at night. Says so right there on the door."

Sterling smacked his chest. She hissed, low enough that only he could hear, "What's wrong with you? That's not how Jake would want you to act. Vaughn was one of his, too."

A low blow. One only a big sister could deliver with such precision. Fine. "I mean, yeah. If you can get away…"

"Like anyone's going to come in tonight anyway." Vaughn

shook his head. "Although I did already get two calls from hands out on your ranch wanting a commemorative tattoo, I don't think I'm ready to do them just yet."

Huh. There was an idea. Bryant tucked it away for later.

"Well, I have about an hour's worth of work left on my custom order. Then I'm heading out that way." Sterling wiped a tear from the corner of her eye. "Viho needs me. But he insisted I not break this contract. So I better hurry."

"Go on, finish up." Bryant hugged her one last time. He let his arms drop to his side, empty. Then he sucked in a huge breath and turned toward Vaughn. "You, too. She's right. Jake would want you there."

Vaughn nodded as if he'd been waiting for Bryant's invitation.

"Tell Mom and Dad I'll be home soon," Sterling said before patting Bryant's chest and walking back toward her shop. She couldn't disguise her sniffle as she went.

"I guess I'll see you tonight then." Vaughn retreated to his door across the sidewalk. He looked over his shoulder one last time before ducking into his place, Cowboy Ink.

For the first time in his life, Bryant wondered what it would be like to let someone—not anyone, but Vaughn specifically—tattoo him. It would be a cheap excuse to lie there and let Vaughn touch him all over...

Ugh.

He obviously hadn't learned a single thing in the six years he'd been gone.

Not a single damn thing.

3

———

Beaten down by grief, annoyance, desperation, and exhaustion, Bryant slid from behind the wheel of his truck. His boots stirred up a cloud of dust that made him aware of how dry it already was at Compass Ranch. He had his work cut out for him.

"Hi, baby." His mom, Cindi, ran out to greet him. She flung herself at him, smothering him in her arms. His father waved from behind her.

"He's hardly a baby anymore," Sam said with a rueful grin as he flung an arm around Bryant's shoulders and another around his mother. "I'm glad you're home, son."

"Thanks, Dad." He shook his head. "Is it really true? It seems like a bad dream."

"I'm afraid so." Sam winced. "I keep expecting him to rip me about leaving my office and getting my hands dirty or insisting we give the workers another raise. It's like I can still hear him and know what he would think about things that are happening, especially of everyone making a big deal over him and his...death. It was that way with JD, and Vicki, too. I guess we carry their influence with us so it's like they're still here, telling us to do the things they would have in real life. They live on in that way, I suppose."

"There was a time when I thought not having a family was the worst thing on earth. Now I realize that the more you hold precious, the more you're opening yourself to be hurt." His mom blinked back tears, making Bryant cringe. She wasn't the crying type. And nothing he said or did could bring Jake back.

Fortunately, his dad knew what she needed to hear. "We loved him as much as we could while he was here. And we'll love him even now that he's not. It'd be far worse to never have met someone worth mourning."

His mom nodded, then tucked herself against his dad's side. She hugged him fiercely and without words Bryant knew what she was thinking. There would come a day when they were separated. His parents. Their kids. All of them. And those days would be dark. They would make the most of the time they had together before then if they were smart.

With a rich history came lots of loss, Bryant realized then. But he knew deep down that Jake and his grandparents wouldn't want them to let their grief eclipse their many blessings, including the progress they could make for future generations, Comptons to come, if they kept the legacy of their ancestors' hard work alive.

"What's all that?" Sam jerked his chin toward the canvas tarps in the back of the truck. They covered some of the equipment Bryant had borrowed from school. "Did you bring home all your stuff? Thought you had a few months to go yet. You're not quitting now, are you?"

"Hell no." Bryant had been looking forward to walking across the stage and claiming his doctoral degree for as long as he could remember. "It's my final project. Or parts of it. Jake... he told me he thought you would approve."

"Then I'm sure I will." His dad nodded. "Can it wait until after the services?"

Although Bryant winced mentally, aware of his approaching deadlines and the need to catch as much rain as possible during the initial phases of the system set up, it didn't feel right to discuss it now. "Yeah, of course. But I'll warn you now, it's going to be expensive."

"So you'll tell me why we should spend a bunch of money on whatever it is you're cooking up. Hopefully it's at least as useful as that still Jake busted you and your cousins cobbling together when you were underage. I'm pretty sure he financed the addition to his house by selling moonshine from that thing. Claimed it was the best he'd ever had."

"That bastard." Bryant laughed. On a ranch, water was more valuable than booze. "It's even better, I promise."

Sam nodded. "I'm looking forward to hearing about it. It'll be nice to have something to work on after..."

Bryant should have known it would be as simple as that. His father trusted him implicitly. Then again, he didn't have all the facts regarding Bryant's poor judgment and the repercussions it could cause, like Jake had. As far as Bryant knew, Jake had never broken his confidence. Had never told his parents why that ranch hand had disappeared so fast, and why Bryant had been so quiet until he too could escape Compton Pass.

Now that his self-imposed banishment was over, he had to come home for longer than a brief visit and deal with reacquainting himself with ranch life and all the restrictions that came with it by himself.

Damn, he missed Jake.

How would he do this on his own?

Simple. The way he had for years now. By ignoring his wayward desires and keeping to himself so he didn't get hurt. He thought of his mom and what she'd said. It was better to be lonely than broken. He knew that now. Next time he saw Vaughn he'd make sure they both understood that so no one, especially not Bryant, got hurt.

Again.

"Uncle Bryant!" His niece Lomasi snapped him from his morose thoughts as she raced out to greet him. At twelve years old, she reminded him so much of Sterling and the way she'd done the same thing when she'd spotted him outside her shop that he couldn't help but grin. Then again, her gray eyes and the wisdom in them reminded him of Jake, her paternal grandfather.

He would see the old man in everything around them.

For a moment that thought struck him hard.

Until he hugged Lomasi tight. "Hey there!"

"You look so sad. Mom said it's okay to cry about Grandpa, but he'd rather you laugh when you think of him." She patted his cheek.

He hoped one day Lomasi and the rest of his nine honorary nieces and nephews—some of whom were technically first cousins once removed, his cousins' kids, not that anyone bothered to make that distinction—might say the same thing about him. For a moment, he pictured the retaining ponds he planned to build and the border landscaping that would help trap water inside the fields. They could be both functional and beautiful.

He vowed to do it right. To contribute what he could to this place they'd all built and continued to improve on together. If he lived well, maybe someday he'd be as loved as Jake. Okay, probably not. But close would be good enough.

"Well, I brought something with me that might cheer you up some." He pivoted and reached into his backpack, which was sitting on the middle of the truck's bench seat. From within he drew out a T-shirt with his college's name and mascot—a bald eagle—printed on it, and handed it to her.

He'd picked it for her because of her love of wildlife. Viho had taught her a lot of his customs. They seemed to resonate with Lomasi more than with her brother and sister.

"This is for me? Really?" Lomasi tugged it on over her dress, then spun in a circle. "I love it! Now we match. I always wanted to be like you."

"Are you kidding?" Bryant rocked back on his heels. He had no idea Lomasi looked up to him in that way. Her admiration swelled his heart and made him wish he'd brought more gifts for her and her siblings.

"Of course." She smiled up at him. "Don't tell Uncle Austin, James, or Doug, but you're my favorite."

Bryant grinned. "Damn straight, I am."

"I won't even tell that you swore. Take a selfie with me?" she asked.

He whipped his phone out of his back pocket and crouched down so they fit in the frame together. For the first time, he saw she resembled him a little around her mouth and nose. Funny that he'd seen everyone else in her instead. Bryant knew then and there that he was home for good, other than defending his thesis and graduation.

Now he just had to figure out how to fit his life into the complex ecosystem of Compass Ranch. It would be harder without Jake's guidance, but not impossible when there were so many people who cared about him around. He couldn't wait to see his cousins at the bonfire later.

Maybe it was time to talk to Austin, Doug, and James about what was really bugging him.

Lomasi put her hand in his and tugged him toward Sterling and Viho's house, where he usually bunked when he was on breaks. They had lived in Sterling's original cottage until they outgrew it and built a full-sized house next door instead. So he often claimed the "guest house".

Maybe he'd talk to Viho and Sterling about renting it from them now that he'd need a place to stay indefinitely. At least until he figured out exactly where to go from here.

4

———

Vaughn wondered if he would go to hell for wrangling an invite to the bonfire being held in Jake's honor with all intentions on seducing Bryant, but he figured the old cowboy would have approved. How many times had he listened to Jake brag about Bryant, talking him up while hinting at things they had in common and all the ways they complemented each other? Vaughn's rebelliousness and Bryant's even keel, Vaughn's promiscuity and Bryant's loyalty, Vaughn's creativity and Bryant's logic. On and on and on.

Even if it was only for a few hot nights, he'd want them to be happy. Yet with one look, it had been plain to see that Bryant wasn't.

And if Vaughn was being honest with himself, neither was he.

Content, sure. Thriving...eh, not really.

He'd gotten comfortable. Lazy. His shop was doing well, and stringless hookups were easy to come by. It had been a while since he'd been *hungry*. And he wasn't talking about that peach pie Mrs. Trapp had added to the pile on the other side of the fire a few minutes ago. He'd bet a night with Bryant would

37

be sweeter than any of the million home-baked goods about to crush that poor folding table covered with a red-and-white checked tablecloth.

Random guys who were mostly interested in sucking his cock in exchange for new ink...well, they had been fun at first. It had gotten old a while ago. He was looking for someone genuine. Someone who was attracted to him for more than what he could do for them—whether that was something artistic or living up to his reputation by giving them a raw, wild fuck.

He was hunting for an actual relationship.

With someone exactly like Bryant Compton.

What had once scared him away—the guy's inexperience and innocence—now drew him like a shaker full of oats in front of one of Seth Compton's prizewinning stallions. A man like Bryant wouldn't sleep with someone for the hell of it. He'd tried that and they both knew it hadn't worked out.

No, he'd only do it if they had a connection. Suddenly, Vaughn found himself wanting to find out if he was good enough. If the spark of attraction that had always existed between them could be fanned very deliberately into something more. And he could only do that if they spent some time together.

So he glanced around, scanning the gathering for golden hair, a quick smile, and the tall, fit body of his prey.

Speak of the stud...

Vaughn leaned up against the cooler and fished a beer from within it. He opened it with his teeth then took a deep drink, trying not to smirk when he noticed Bryant staring at his throat. It flexed while his lips wrapped around the opening of the bottle. He needed the long pull to cool himself off. It was crazy how being near Bryant made him feel like one of the logs on the bonfire, about to combust at any moment.

He'd gladly blow Bryant's mind…and cock…if given half a chance.

Though they might have stayed put, sizing each other up without speaking the rest of the night if left to their own devices, James Compton—completely oblivious to the history, present, and hopefully the future, between him and Bryant—called, "Hey, Vaughn!"

He tried to remain pleasant as he chatted with Austin about the new ink he wanted, except all he could see was Bryant. Which was why he noticed the nearly imperceptible tightening of the guy's lips and the tension around his eyes when Hayden mentioned that it was almost time for him to graduate. The grooves there deepened as he explained what he was doing back home and that he planned to stay for at least a while.

Part of Vaughn cheered at the thought of having Bryant so close, for longer than a day or two. Maybe forever, if he stayed after finally finishing school.

The other part was worried for the guy. His gut told him there was more causing Bryant to wring his hands than Jake's passing. He was stressed the fuck out. Vaughn would be glad to provide a little relief. For them both. "Maybe your problem is that you work too much, Bryant. I remember lots of times in the past few years that Jake told me he'd had to lecture you again about cutting loose and having some fun. In his memory, I'd be willing to help you out with that."

His impure intentions must have been obscenely obvious.

Bryant's cousin Doug grinned, while James and even Austin nodded in agreement.

At least the three of them were on his side. The girls they'd brought home, too, if Hayden and Ivy's approving smirks were any indication. Unfortunately, they weren't the person he was trying to persuade. Hell no, he had to go and pick the most stubborn one of the bunch.

"You know I don't date cowboys." Bryant crossed his arms,

only making the muscles in them and his chest more prominent. That was definitely not deterrent for Vaughn. Neither was Bryant's glower.

"I always thought that was a stupid rule," Vaughn replied. Inside he appended, *Besides...I'm not a cowboy anymore. I'm an artist. I was only doing what I had to in order to survive at that point in my life.*

He'd be sure to show Bryant the difference sometime.

Vaughn got pulled deeper into his side conversation with Austin about doing a major addition to his back, potentially including a memorial portrait of Jake. While they hashed it out, Bryant flushed and turned to Doug and James, acting for all the world like whatever they were talking about was fascinating.

But Vaughn had no intentions of letting him off that easy. Though he drifted off after he'd finished making plans for an official consultation with Austin, he stood nearby, shooting the shit with a lot of the guys he knew from his days working the ranch or from their patronage of his shop. He had no shortage of friends in Compton Pass.

One less than he'd had the day before.

Shit. Jake's really gone.

It hit him hard right then—that this wasn't somebody's birthday bash and he would never see Jake again. Just like his father, Jake had died before Vaughn had said everything he should have. A mistake he would be sure never to make again. If there was someone he cared about, they'd know it.

He stumbled away to lean against a tree on the fringes of the amber light cast by the roaring flames. Ragged breaths made his chest saw in and out painfully.

"Hey. Are *you* okay?" Bryant's fingers squeezed Vaughn's shoulder. When was the last time a guy had given a fuck about how he felt? Never, that's when.

He shrugged, loving the comforting weight of Bryant's fingers there when he did. With any other guy, he'd struggle to admit that, even to himself. But with Bryant, it felt okay. He was harmless. He was kind. He was sincere. This wasn't some ploy to get to him, so it made it easier to be honest in return. "You know. It seems normal for a while, and then…"

"You remember he's dead. Yeah, I do know." Bryant hung his head. "I'm sorry I was such a douche before. I know you're hurting, too. Everyone here is."

"That's true, but just because we share one wound doesn't mean anyone else understands your other scars. I didn't mean to trample on those, although I think I might have somehow." It was a first for him. Actually caring about how a man felt other than making sure he was satisfied in bed. Vaughn wasn't sure how to do this, so he just tried his best and hoped it was enough.

"Well, yeah. That and I guess I've been holding a grudge all this time. That's not right either. I'll do my best to get over that ancient shit. It's just that coming back home… It's tough. For a lot of reasons."

"I'm sorry, too." Vaughn took a deep breath, filling his lungs with the scent of leather and fresh air that he associated with Bryant. "Before we put it behind us for good, I need to say something. I should have protected you that day. It's partly my fault…what happened to you, I mean. It's bothered me ever since that I left you alone with that asshole."

"What?" Bryant looked as if he might haul off and sucker punch Vaughn. "How could you say that? I didn't need you to *protect* me, you son of a bitch. I needed you to *want* me."

Vaughn jerked back as if Bryant had actually hit him. He couldn't have been more surprised. "What the hell makes you think I didn't?"

"The fact that you turned me down flat." Bryant sneered, letting Vaughn see what was probably only a fraction of his turmoil. "I get it. Honestly, I do. You wanted someone who was worth messing with. And I wasn't. Not at the risk of your job. I probably wouldn't be very good in the sack. I mean, *wouldn't have been* and you knew it. That's why you told me I wasn't ready. Taunting me made me think maybe...if I fooled around with someone else..."

Vaughn narrowed his eyes. Both at Bryant's slip of the tongue and the absolute ludicrousness of what he was saying then.

"You've got it all fucked up. I was trying to do the right thing. End of story. You were a minor, for Christ's sake, and the stuff I wanted to do to you was definitely illegal." He leaned in closer, wishing he could give Bryant a demonstration of how hard he'd been for hours straight—since he'd seen Bryant in town again and lots of nights in between—as he imagined how differently things might have gone if they'd run into each other a few months later than they had.

Bryant laughed. It wasn't a fun sound, though. It was strained and tattered. "So you did it for my own good, is that it? Whatever you need to tell yourself, Vaughn. You don't need to let me down easy anymore. At least I'm being honest here."

Vaughn glanced around, finding everyone else engaged either in conversation or stuffing their faces. He gripped Bryant by the collar and dragged him into what most Comptons referred to as Vivi's Garden. The verdant foliage stretched out beside the main house. It had grown over the years into a veritable jungle of vegetables and flowers. Every year the bounty from Vivi's Garden took first place in the county fair. In fact, they'd even named the competition after Bryant's grandmother and the entry fees were donated to Alzheimer's research organizations in her name.

Lost in the center of the lush vegetation, they were invisible to anyone else. Though the voices and the crackle of the fire carried through the plants, no one could spy on them. Which was good because Vaughn was about to teach his book-smart obsession a lesson in dangerous attractions.

He whipped around and trapped Bryant against a trellis, monitoring him carefully. The only sign of shock was the dilation of his pupils. He didn't tense or spook. "Are you calling me a liar?"

"I'm saying you're being generous, and looking at the past through rose-colored glasses." Bryant didn't flinch when Vaughn inched closer. Soon their chests would be plastered together and Bryant would have no doubt that Vaughn wanted him. His hard cock would communicate his desire plain enough.

He watched in case any lingering demons reared their heads. The last thing he'd ever want to do was trigger Bryant, reminding him of the dark parts of their shared past instead of what could be a very bright spot in their near futures.

He had to be transparent if Bryant was going to believe him and change what seemed to be some deep-seated misconceptions. "Look, I admit I wasn't thrilled when I realized how inexperienced you were. But that's only because I didn't want to be the one to corrupt you. Not because I thought you were lacking in any way whatsoever. The mere sight of you turns me on. Always has. It wasn't easy doing my job with a stiff cock all the time. I was afraid Jake would notice and fire my ass. I *needed* that fucking job."

When Bryant made some indistinct sound of disbelief from deep in his chest, Vaughn only knew one way to convince him. He took Bryant's hand and pressed it to his crotch, where even now, their proximity was creating a situation his tight jeans weren't well equipped to handle.

"This is for me?" Bryant whispered.

"Yeah," he growled when Bryant's fingers began to explore, measuring him with the brush of his thumb along Vaughn's length. The last thing he intended to do was squash Bryant's curiosity. "Don't worry, I've got plenty to show you a good time, if you'll let me. I want to make up for what happened back when we were too young to do it right. I know a fuck-ton more now. Trust me. You're getting the better end of the deal. It will have been worth our wait."

Vaughn wasn't sure what he said, but Bryant froze. He went stiff where he'd been pliant, and not in a good way either. "Well, I'm not sure I've done as much maturing as you have."

With his palms flat on Vaughn's chest, Bryant shoved him backwards.

He hadn't been trying to hold the guy against his will. No, he wanted Brainy Compton to come willingly to his bed, which was where he knew they were going to end up sooner or later.

It would be impossible to have this much attraction arcing between them and ignore it unless they were separated by several states, as they had been for years. It was strong enough to make Vaughn regret, for the first time in his life, that he hadn't been cut out for higher education.

Still, Bryant's denial shocked him. He couldn't remember the last time a man had turned him down when he'd shown interest in them. Bryant would never do what Vaughn expected. He needed to remember that. Making that mistake had cost them both dearly once. He wouldn't allow it to happen again.

"I'm not sure how I screwed up just now. But when you're willing to tell me, and help me give you what you want, I hope you'll come find me." Vaughn tipped his hat and prepared to leave.

But he couldn't stop himself from stealing a single kiss.

The kiss he hadn't dared to take back when they were still kids.

Even more, he wanted to give one to Bryant in the hopes that it could make up for what he'd withheld in the past. That simple gesture might have been enough to prevent tragedy, though Vaughn was fairly certain he hadn't had enough self-control to stop with a kiss back then.

He prayed he did now.

"Just so you don't doubt what I told you when you walk away tonight..." He reached out and speared his hands into Bryant's longish blond locks, then swooped in. He wasn't rough or rushed. Definitely not forceful or cruel. Instead, he sipped from Bryant's lips, savoring the taste of something chocolate the man had indulged in from the dessert pile.

It tasted a thousand times better mixed with the flavor of geek.

Bryant shivered in his grip, then moaned. He took hold of Vaughn, clinging to him every bit as much as Vaughn was clutching Bryant. He opened his mouth and allowed Vaughn to explore with his tongue and lips.

For a few minutes, Vaughn was able to forget the pain of loss—losing Jake, the time he'd lost with Bryant, and the innocence Bryant had lost that day in the barn. Instead, his world was filled with the joy of creating something instead.

Like when he drew, his brain was filled with possibilities.

He cradled Bryant's head between his hands, directing him so that he angled his face to best accept Vaughn's kiss. He held him in place as he made love to Bryant's mouth. He sucked lightly on Bryant's lower lip before flicking his tongue over it, wishing it were as easy or effective to salve the rest of Bryant's soul.

The longer they kissed, the better it got. Each of them gave in a little until they met in the middle, open and receptive to the sweet and spicy exchange. Vaughn relaxed, enjoying the moment. He felt the muscles beneath his fingertips do the same. Bryant rested against the trellis, no longer poised to bolt.

So Vaughn stepped in. Their chests collided, pressing together in all the right ways. It was unusual for Vaughn to be with a man taller than himself, but he found he got off on knowing he was still able to take control of someone larger, someone better than him in every sense, and make it good for them.

He had prepared to mentor Bryant in what he liked.

It turned out Bryant Compton was one hell of a kisser. He made out like he did most everything in life, as far as Vaughn could tell. He committed one-hundred percent. Like he had when he'd refused to settle for less than a doctorate degree or when he'd driven all night to get home after a family emergency.

That kind of dedication spurred Vaughn on. He had to match Bryant's passion. Their quiet, soothing kiss began to escalate. Bryant's hands wandered down Vaughn's back to his ass. He gave a surprised grunt when long fingers slipped into the back pockets of his jeans and squeezed.

Vaughn parted Bryant's lips and began to explore with his teeth and tongue.

He one-upped Bryant's bold grip by sliding his hands under Bryant's shirt and running the flat of his palm up Bryant's sides. Bryant shivered, then went slack. Vaughn could have done anything then and Bryant wouldn't have objected, he was pretty sure.

Instead of taking advantage of the situation and the vulnerability Bryant had shown him, Vaughn backed off. He clutched Bryant to him, hugging him tight as he slowly eased the pressure of their mouths, which had only moments earlier been crushed together.

When their lips separated, Bryant groaned. Vaughn's dick jerked in his pants.

Neither of them moved, though Vaughn was dying to peer into Bryant's eyes and read whatever might be in them. So he took a breath that was shakier than a simple kiss should make it. Then he pried open his eyes and looked.

Bryant was staring right back, a mixture of shock and gratitude radiating from him.

Vaughn didn't really understand that. After all, he was the one who was grateful for Bryant. The guy had woken something he hadn't realized was dormant. Something fierce and unshakeable.

From the pulse hammering in Bryant's neck, Vaughn thought he wasn't the only one having a revelation at the moment. He felt pretty smug about how things had gone, and his eventual victory in their steer-and-cowboy game.

Until Bryant's parting shot. He pushed past Vaughn, who was still dazed with pleasure and let him have it. "You said you were trying to protect me then. We both know how that turned out. Why should I believe this time would be any different?"

Vaughn couldn't believe he had to ask. "Because I'd never disrespect you like that motherfucker did. I'd never hurt you or use you or put my pleasure above yours."

"Yeah, but one of us—and I'm pretty sure it's me—is going to be crushed when the other gets tired of this diversion. You should know I'm planning on staying in Compton Pass. This wouldn't be a random anonymous affair. We'd have to see each other all the time and...remember. Is that really what you're signing up for? Because I'm not sure I can handle that. There are enough landmines around Compton Pass for my liking."

Vaughn's arms ached to hold Bryant again. Except this time to ease the pain he could see in the other man's eyes.

But he knew this wasn't his chance. Bryant had already reached his limit for the night. It was a lot to take in. Their attraction even rocked him, jaded though he might have been.

"I'm glad to hear you're hanging around. I know you don't believe me, but what I said tonight is true. Think about it. I'm not a quitter and I suspect that if you ask yourself what you really want, when no one is looking to judge you, you're going to be knocking on my door sooner rather than later. I can't wait for that day and I'm going to have fun chasing you until you give in to what I know we both need."

"You're an arrogant son of a bitch, you know that?"

"That's confidence, Bryant. I'm sure that I'm right. And I'm willing to prove it. Whenever you're finally ready."

At that last phrase, Bryant winced. His face turned red, and not from arousal.

Too late, Vaughn remembered how he'd told Bryant he wasn't ready that day in the barn. Right before everything had gone to hell. In fact, he'd practically dared Bryant to fool around with that sack of shit or whoever came along after him, even if he hadn't realized it back then.

Fuck.

Before Vaughn could fix things, Bryant shook his head and spun on his heels. This time he didn't look back or stop when Vaughn called his name. He marched out to the fire and rejoined his cousins in the warmth and light.

Vaughn went home alone...that night.

5

Vaughn had thought entirely too much about Bryant and their exchange the night before. In fact, he'd been consumed by his missteps. Especially while he'd carefully watched Bryant and his cousins at Jake's services that afternoon. Their heavy hearts had been obvious despite their best attempts to remember all the good times they'd shared with the man they'd obviously cared deeply for.

Bryant didn't need Vaughn making his life more difficult.

Vaughn had screwed up. Again.

Since he couldn't think of anything else anyway, he figured he might as well come over and try to make up for it. Otherwise regret would eat him up like the mosquitos that came out in the summer. A bite here, a bite there, until he couldn't stand to live in his skin anymore.

So he'd decided to hang around Compass Ranch and offer his support in the hopes he could start to make things right between them. If Bryant told him to get the hell away, he'd do that, too.

He spread his legs and prepared to camp out as long as necessary to catch Bryant leaving his family gathering, which had followed Jake's funeral. During the ceremony, one filled with touching stories and even some laughter, Vaughn had studied Bryant to distract himself from his own sorrow. Therefore, he had noticed each of the thirty-seven times the guy flicked his gaze in Vaughn's direction, not-so-covertly checking him out.

Lying in wait now, he felt a little like a creeper but more like someone determined to do what he knew was best for them both. Even if Bryant didn't yet agree.

He'd probably been standing there for over an hour when he saw Bryant's cousin, James, and the pretty girl, Ivy, from James's smoke jumping base who'd accompanied him. Though he'd introduced her as his friend, Vaughn wasn't blind. Those two were going to be as solid as any of the rest of the Compass clan. That was one thing about them. They mated for life. He couldn't think of a single Compton who hadn't stuck by their woman, or man, or men, once they'd fallen in love.

Would Bryant be that faithful to the man he finally gave his heart to?

Vaughn hoped so. That was another quality that was in short supply in his circle of hookups. Here today, gone tomorrow. Nothing more than the current moment was expected.

Vaughn wanted someone he could count on. The kind of guy he could talk to about his day and life in general. Something beyond how he liked to be fucked or what kind of ink he wanted next.

Where he'd struggled to get excited about tattooing another barbed wire armband on random cowboys, Bryant inspired lots of design ideas. To pass the time, Vaughn imagined what he might draw on that creamy skin, which would make an incredible canvas. He'd shape the lines around the contours of Bryant's smoking hot body.

As far as he knew, Bryant didn't have any tattoos. Vaughn

was more than willing to do a personal check to confirm his suspicions. Lost in thoughts of inspecting every inch of Bryant, preferably with his mouth and tongue, he didn't realize the door had opened quietly until the porch steps creaked as someone descended.

"What are you doing here?" Bryant asked, tipping his head slightly to one side as he approached Vaughn and his truck.

"You're the whiz kid. What do you think?" Vaughn smiled, hopeful that Bryant would take his response as the compliment it was. He'd been called a lot of things in his life—sexy, hardworking, and one hell of a fuck—but a brainiac wasn't one of them. Bryant was legendary around the ranch and the town in general. Hell, he'd gotten a perfect score on his SATs and started taking college-level classes when he was still a junior in high school.

How was Vaughn supposed to talk with someone like that? Probably he'd be dull to Bryant. Maybe he'd wasted his time. Confused them both. Made an awkward situation unbearable.

When Bryant smiled in return, all his doubts vanished. "I'm guessing you're not delivering ice cream or coming to shovel shit like you used to."

"Do you want ice cream?" Good to know Bryant had a sweet tooth. That info could come in handy sometime. "Would that make you less pissed at me for being such a dumbass last night?"

"You know, I haven't had King Cone in years. Is the stand open yet?" Bryant stood straighter and walked faster at the mention of a double scoop. Vaughn tried desperately not to think of what they could do in bed with some chocolate syrup and whipped cream after polishing off dessert.

Fortunately, he knew the answer to Bryant's question. "Yup. I stopped there just the other night for a milkshake on my way into the shop. Can I take you out for some?"

"As in a date?" Bryant wondered.

"Yeah, sure. If that's what you want to call it." He shrugged. "Mostly I just want to catch up. Find out what your life has been like since I knew you before. And maybe try to convince you that I'm not the asshole you think I am."

"I don't—"

"Hey, I didn't give you a lot of reason to believe otherwise last night. I'm sorry about that. I guess I underestimated how what happened back then still affects you now. And once I figured it out, I felt pretty shitty about my part in it. I know ice cream doesn't count for much…"

"A lot of problems could be solved with ice cream." Bryant flashed his dimples as he climbed into the cab. "Get in, Vaughn. I'm hungry."

"Me too," he murmured under his breath as he jogged around the hood and boosted himself into the passenger seat of Bryant's truck. Both of them understood there was no way Bryant had left his aunt's house anything less than stuffed, but he was giving Vaughn this shot anyway.

Maybe he wanted to rewrite history as badly as Vaughn did.

He could hope.

They rode without saying anything for a while, long enough that Vaughn wondered if they'd ever speak or if Bryant would just keep driving until he reached the ice cream stand, bought himself a treat, then went back home. As if Vaughn was some phantom hitching a ride.

Eventually, he couldn't stand it anymore. "Are you still pissed about last night?"

"Nah. I'm not the kind of person to stay angry. I guess I'm just…wrung out. Overwhelmed and exhausted." Bryant sighed.

Vaughn covered Bryant's free hand, which rested on his thigh, and squeezed. "If this is too much, turn around. That's fine."

"Oh no, I'm getting some damn ice cream. You put that idea in my head—now it sounds really good." He glanced over with a wicked grin that reminded Vaughn of the boy he used to be. "Besides, I feel like torturing you by making you watch me lick it."

Vaughn groaned. Maybe he should have thought harder about his plan.

When Bryant laughed, he figured the torture would be worth it.

They rolled up to the stand and placed their orders. When Becky Sue told them how much it would be, Vaughn whipped out his wallet. He ordinarily wasn't a super traditional guy, but he wanted Bryant to realize he'd made something of himself. Okay, so most anyone could afford a couple of ice cream cones, but truth was, there'd been a time when Vaughn wasn't one of them.

"You didn't have to do that. But...thanks." Bryant smiled and gave his ice cream a long lick from the cone to the tip. Vaughn's cock noticed, and approved. Damn.

Bryant laughed again as he sauntered to a picnic table nearby and straddled the bench. Vaughn took a seat just past Bryant's knees, with his back resting against the table.

After a few minutes of dedicated eating, complete with incredible soft hums from Bryant—which Vaughn could easily repurpose in his imagination as sounds he'd make when they were fooling around—Bryant asked, "Where are *your* tattoos?"

Vaughn glanced down at his bare arms and braced himself for Bryant's mockery. He clenched his jaw, then spat, "Don't have any."

"Isn't it weird for a tattoo artist not to have any tattoos?" Bryant wondered without laughing.

"Probably." Vaughn forced himself to relax, took a bite from his cone, and then tried to explain. "Every day I do cover-ups and draw dumb shit people will regret eventually. I'm going to get tattooed someday. I'm just waiting for the right thing. The absolute perfect thing. Until then...I can wait."

"I respect that," Bryant said when most people would have shaken their head or called him some kind of hypocrite. Hell, plenty of guys had before. "When you're looking for a forever thing, it's better to be sure."

Vaughn wondered what Bryant was waiting for. As far as he knew, the guy had never had a serious boyfriend. Maybe that was what he meant. It wasn't worth the hassle of bringing someone home and introducing them to the millions of Comptons swarming Compass Ranch until it was the perfect somebody.

If they hooked up, would Bryant keep it a secret, too?

Somehow that didn't sit right with Vaughn. He wanted everyone to know he'd staked a claim.

Something in his expression must have tipped Bryant off to his thoughts. "Settle down, Vaughn. I wasn't referring to you. I was talking about myself. Anyway, never mind." He flashed a lopsided smile. "You remind me a lot of your dad. Direct, kinder than you think under a tough exterior, a badass artist, a little moody, you know?"

At least he'd included the art thing. It was the one trait Vaughn was grateful he'd inherited from Snake.

"The truth is, you knew my dad better than I did." Vaughn shrugged one shoulder. Still, it touched something deep inside him to know Bryant thought so. "I never had that tight bond, like you do, with your family. My mom does the best she can, but she's not like yours. Her focus was never me. She worked a lot of nights, and partied hard, even after having me by mistake with a cowboy just passing through for the rodeo. She told me not to worry because she'd gotten her tubes tied after that little surprise. It took her a few years to track Snake down, and by then he was already older. He always provided for me, or thought he did, but my mom used a lot of that cash on getting her nails done, or making her hair bigger, always in the hopes of snagging some rich guy. As if there were billionaires pouring through the doors of the shithole bar where she waited tables.

"It was probably around the time that Jake found Viho that my dad started bringing me up here for the summers. At first, it was awkward as shit. I was a punk and didn't handle it well. I was used to essentially being on my own and he had a hell of a lot of rules. Then, just about the time we'd sort through all that each summer, I had to go back. When I came up here for good, at the end, Snake made a real effort. But it was too late. It was impossible for me to get attached knowing I was only going to lose him. The last thing he said to me was that I was his biggest regret."

Vaughn figured his relationship with his dad, and putting Bryant in a situation where he got hurt, had to top his own list. So that seemed fair enough. At least he had a chance to make amends to one of the important people he'd disappointed now.

"I'm sure he meant not bringing you to Compass Ranch to live sooner was a mistake." Bryant didn't hesitate on that one.

"I think so too, now. Jake helped me see that was probably true. But I guess we'll never know for sure. He fell into unconsciousness soon after and never woke up." Vaughn scrubbed his hands over his face. "Shit. Not sure why I'm telling you all that. I guess Jake...it's bringing those memories to the surface."

Bryant scooted closer and put his hand on Vaughn's knee. "I'm sorry, that sucks. I can't imagine growing up without my family. They're loud, and overwhelming sometimes, but I always knew they were there for me. That they love me unconditionally."

"Then why didn't you tell your cousins about what happened in the barn that summer?" Vaughn asked before he could think better of it.

Bryant choked on the last bite of his ice cream cone. He

took longer than necessary to wipe his mouth on a tissue-thin napkin, then said, "How do you know I didn't?"

"Because they never would have let you keep blaming yourself like you do. You'd have dealt with it better and moved on by now, I'm guessing."

Bryant didn't bother to deny it. He looked down at his boots. "I don't know. It's weird being the only gay guy in the bunch. They don't get some things. They try. They're accepting of me. It's just not part of their experience, you know? And they've certainly never been overpowered by one of their dates. I guess I didn't think they'd really understand."

"And you were ashamed." Vaughn tried not to get angry. It took every ounce of his self-control not to ball his fists or shout at the injustice of it all. He didn't want Bryant to misinterpret his emotions.

"Of course." Bryant looked around to see if anyone was listening. They weren't. No one gave a shit about what two random dudes were saying. If anything, there were several women eying them up hopefully. Sorry, ladies. "Can we talk about something else?"

Vaughn was sure now that Bryant still needed help dealing with what had happened.

He wasn't positive he was equipped to handle it, but he planned to try.

It was the least he could do to make up for his part in the situation.

"Sure. Are you staying out at Sterling's place?" Vaughn wondered. Would his sister notice if Bryant didn't go back to the cottage behind the beautiful house she and Viho had built for their family? And if she did, would she care?

Vaughn had gotten to know her pretty well, since their shops were so close. She'd bring him coffee in the afternoons when she was winding down and he was gearing up for the busy evening shift. He'd even done a few tats on her—her kids' names. Pretty, understated. They'd stand the test of time because they meant something. Exactly the sort of thing that would make him go under the gun.

He kind of thought Sterling would give him the thumbs-up. Then again, she was fiercely protective of her baby brother. Just like every other Compton. They looked out for their own. It was probably for the best that Bryant had never told his father—or hell, his uncle Silas—about what had happened. They'd probably have done something violent and gotten themselves in trouble.

"Yeah. Yeah, I am." Bryant sighed. "I guess I should be heading back there before she gets worried. Besides, I'm pretty wrecked after today."

It wasn't a super-long ride out to Compass Ranch from town, but there were plenty of wild animals that liked to jump into the road and sharp turns could catch him off guard in the dark. Especially if he wasn't used to the trip at night, having been away so much of the past six years.

"You know, my place is on the way if you're not up for the drive." Vaughn tried to remain casual, though everything inside him wanted to pick Bryant up, put him over his shoulder, and cart him off right then and there. That probably wouldn't go well since Bryant was actually broader and taller than him and had learned how to scrap with the rest of the Compass Boys, who were no pushovers.

Just because Bryant was less of a hothead than James and less rowdy than Doug or Austin didn't mean he wasn't capable of protecting himself. Vaughn had been shocked, and turned on, the first time he'd seen Bryant after he'd moved away. He'd clearly made physical fitness a priority despite the time he spent with his nose in a book.

Vaughn wondered if it was precisely so that Bryant could fight back hard if he ever had to again.

"Where *do* you live?" Bryant asked, cutting off Vaughn's train of thought.

"Above my shop. I built an apartment there. It's not huge or fancy or anything, but it suits my needs."

"Short commute, too. Can't beat that." Bryant should know —him and all his family lived on the ranch they worked. Although the damn thing was big enough that it could take a while to get from one section to another, especially if going on horseback, which they sometimes did.

"Yeah." Vaughn nodded. "I don't get to ride my horse to work, but I sometimes slide down the bannister when no one's looking."

Bryant chuckled. "Well, since we're so close, want me to drop you off? You could catch a ride out with Sterling to pick up your truck tomorrow. Or I could have one of the hands drive it back to you."

Vaughn cleared his throat and took his time wiping the last of the ice cream from his face with the shitty napkin. His chance was slipping away. He could feel it. And the last thing he wanted was for Bryant to rebuild the wall between them. "Or...you could stay over and we could ride out to Compass Ranch together in the morning so I could pick up my truck."

"Uh..." Bryant looked around, as if searching for a graceful exit where there was none.

With any other guy, Vaughn would know how to handle the situation. He'd picked up plenty of men. Enough to have it down to a science. With Bryant, he had to be careful. Thoughtful. The kind of guy worthy of having him, if only for a night.

"Look, Bryant, while I'd like nothing more than to pull some alpha bullshit, grab your keys and tell you I'm not taking no for an answer...." Vaughn shook his head. "That's not how I roll. And I don't think that's what you need. I want you to come home with me. But if you're not ready—"

Bryant growled like he'd rip Vaughn's throat out if he said that again.

"It's not a bad thing!" Vaughn put his hands up. "No worries if you're not. I'll ask you again tomorrow. And the next day. And the next day. Feel free to tell me no as many times as you like. You won't hurt my feelings or keep me from trying again. Unless you tell me you don't want me to do that either. But I hope you won't."

Bryant chugged a bottle of water he'd bought as if his mouth had gotten parched at the thought of tearing up his sheets. "I don't know what I want, Vaughn. That's the honest truth. There are so many things running through my mind right now, I can't process them all."

"I get that." How many times had Vaughn waffled between heartache and lust in the past day? It was a weird combination. "You don't have to decide right now. Just come with me. We'll talk, hang out, chill, and if something more comes of it, fine. If not, at least neither of us will have to be alone tonight."

Bryant blinked as he considered. "You really won't be disappointed if all I want to do is crash on your couch later? I'm not trying to lead you on. I need to be really clear about that, okay? Tell me you understand."

Lead him on? Why did that sound like bullshit leftover from years ago? Was Bryant still struggling with what his abuser had claimed that day? How he'd tried victim-blaming in an effort to keep from being slaughtered by a herd of loyal cowboys? Could Bryant still believe even a shred of what that loser had said was true?

Vaughn narrowed his eyes, concentrated on keeping his fingers loose and unfisted, then said, "I understand. Perfectly."

"Okay." Bryant nodded.

"Okay?"

"Did you really think I would turn you down?" He smiled

shyly, making every one of Vaughn's primal instincts roar to life. "It killed me to do it last night. I've wanted this for years."

"Me too." Vaughn groaned. "Why the hell did you have to pick a college so far away?"

"I guess you were right that day. I wasn't ready. More so after... So I put myself out of range." He shrugged.

Vaughn squeezed Bryant's knee. "Do you know that you're safe with me?"

"Yeah." He paused. "I guess I'm just wondering...why would you bother? I'm a pain in the ass. Complicated. Surely you've had a bunch of boyfriends since then. You could choose anyone. Why me?"

Vaughn figured the least he could do was be as honest as Bryant was being, even if it made him a little uncomfortable to admit it. "Plenty of sex, sure. Boyfriends, no. Not really."

"Oh. Is that what you're looking for now? Otherwise, it makes even less sense. Why would you pick me to sleep with when there are lots of other men in this town who know what to do with a man like you and would jump at the chance?" Bryant cleared his throat when he referred to fucking around, making Vaughn realize that he still didn't have much experience. Damn, wasn't that what college was for? That's what it looked like on TV, anyway.

It figured Bryant was the one guy who went all study and no play. The urge to help him unwind grew until it was as big of a motivator as Vaughn's rock-solid cock.

"I've always found you attractive on the outside." Vaughn trailed his knuckles over Bryant's cheek then down his jaw. "Now that I'm getting to know you, you're only getting hotter to me."

"Same goes." Bryant stood up and shocked Vaughn by holding out his hand. Not just to help him up, as he first suspected when he placed his palm in Bryant's. No, he didn't let go even after Vaughn was standing beside him. Instead, he led Vaughn to his truck and opened the door for him.

That was a first for Vaughn. And he'd be lying if he said he didn't get off on it. "I like that you're different from the other guys I've been with. You're special, Bryant. Don't ever let someone make you doubt that."

Though he didn't say anything, Bryant turned to him with a smile that transformed him from smoldering to irresistibly sexy. Vaughn had finally said the right thing.

They couldn't make it to his place fast enough.

6

———

Bryant climbed the metal stairs at the back of Cowboy Ink while staring at Vaughn's tight ass in his perfectly cut jeans. He'd give all the water in the Indian Ocean to see what was beneath that denim. Was pretty sure that if he asked, Vaughn would show him this time. And still, he was too afraid to open his mouth and admit he craved a taste of this man even more than the vanilla-chocolate swirl they'd devoured.

He followed Vaughn, who seemed more willing to listen than he had been in the past.

And that's when Bryant realized it.

Vaughn had grown. Matured. While Bryant was still standing still, stuck in the same spot he'd been in since their lives had last crossed paths. He hated that about himself.

Maybe it was time to do something about it. To unfreeze his emotions and desires.

Sure, he was progressing on a professional level, but personally...not so much. Bryant steeled himself for the night ahead and hoped whatever happened would help him take the first steps forward. If he was going to do that, he had to explain the situation to Vaughn. *Fuck.*

He did believe he was in good hands with Vaughn. But it was still hard to talk about.

Just about the time he got ready to spill his guts, Vaughn unlocked the door to his apartment and ushered Bryant inside. Whatever he'd been about to say got stuck in his throat when he took in the sleek, masculine apartment. It looked nothing like the rest of Compton Pass.

Completely out of place in their tiny country town. Just like Bryant.

There wasn't a hint of shiplap or a single quilt or distressed anything. Instead, it was all gray tile floors and honed black granite counters. Stainless steel appliances and high efficiency fixtures. Straight-line, simple furniture. Modern. Sexy as fuck.

"Wow," Bryant muttered as he kicked off his boots at the door, then turned in a circle, loving the open-concept floor plan. Though he couldn't see it at night, he was sure the giant windows on the rear wall of the apartment provided a glorious view of the surrounding mountains. It was exactly like something he'd want for himself. He took mental notes. He'd either need to renovate Sterling's cottage or build something of his own if he was going to stay on the ranch long-term. Something like this would be ideal. "This place is..."

"Small, I know." Vaughn winced. "But it's just me. No need for anything extravagant."

"You made great use of the space. It's perfect." Bryant's eyes were drawn immediately to a charge controller discreetly concealed behind a smoky glass panel. "Is this for solar?"

"Yep. Not so useful in the winter, but this time of year I can get most of my power from the roof." Vaughn shrugged. "Seems like a no-brainer to me. I also installed a catchment system to make use of runoff for the landscaping in front of the shop, and the toilet, and stuff."

And...Bryant was officially in lust. Eco-friendly, knew his way around the bedroom, not quite a cowboy but still full of swagger? Oh yeah. Vaughn was the one. He'd always been the one.

Bryant refused to miss out on another chance with him.

But first he had to come clean about his lack of experience so Vaughn knew what he was getting into, and so he knew to take it easy on Bryant...at least at first. Hopefully Vaughn wouldn't change his mind if he knew just how fucked up Bryant was.

Vaughn took him for a brief tour, though most of the area was on display. "If you need to use the bathroom, the only one is in here, through my bedroom. Sorry, I didn't really think of having guests when I designed the layout."

Bryant knew what he really meant. He'd assumed anyone sleeping over would share his bed. Well, hopefully, Bryant wouldn't be the first to break the streak. "I'd rather stay with you anyway. If that's okay."

Vaughn blinked. "Of course. I just thought... I mean, I'm not trying to push you into anything you're not comfortable with."

"We both know that's not what you're doing. I've been in that situation. It was nothing like this." Bryant cleared his throat, prepared to lay himself bare. In fact, he was kind of looking forward to it. For years, he hadn't had anyone who understood where he was coming from or why he was so damn cautious about finding a lover. "Back when that happened, you know..."

Damn, this was harder than he thought. He took a shaky breath, but Vaughn beat him to it. "When that child molester attacked you?"

"Well, when you put it like that it sounds a lot worse."

"Worse than what, exactly?" Vaughn turned to face Bryant. "How do you think about what happened that day in your own mind?"

"I was butt-hurt when you turned me down. Because of that, I made a terrible decision. I just wanted a kiss. To know what it felt like to make out with a man. Instead, it was a disaster of a hookup."

"That's completely crazy. Bryant, that asshole was on the prowl for someone susceptible to his manipulation. When he found you, he pounced. He lured you in so he could *rape* you. Plain and simple. That's what he fucking did." Vaughn's teeth were clenched. The veins in his neck bulged.

Bryant had never thought of it like that. Definitely had never considered the R word in regards to himself. Was that what had happened? Things had gotten out of hand, sure. But rape? He reflexively waved Vaughn off. "Not exactly."

"Did you at any time say no?" Vaughn asked matter-of-factly. "I don't care what you said or how it started out. At some point, did you tell him you weren't into it?"

Bryant nodded.

"Did he stop?"

Bryant shook his head. They both knew he hadn't.

"Shit, if I hadn't left you there alone that day, it wouldn't have happened. If you want to blame anyone, it should be me. Not yourself. I relived that moment—the one where one of the hands said they'd heard Bill grunting and you screaming then saw Jake charge in there, or the one where I saw your face and the blood on your clothes after and realized what had happened—a million times in my nightmares, but I can never change it. I'd give anything to go back..."

"What?" Bryant whipped his stare to Vaughn.

His tortured gaze ripped Bryant open.

Had Vaughn suffered because of that bastard, too? He'd never imagined the other guy might have been beating himself up or he would have reached out to put his mind at ease. Bryant didn't blame Vaughn. Not one bit. He shouldn't blame himself for the actions of a despicable bastard.

In that moment, Bryant had an epiphany: Jake had been absolutely right. If he was willing to absolve Vaughn of any guilt in the situation, maybe he too had been a victim, not responsible for Bill's vile actions.

In that instant, he became a million pounds lighter. Vaughn had helped him without even realizing it. "Maybe we've both been too hard on ourselves."

"Could be. I think it's time we fixed the mistakes we made that day." Vaughn ran his knuckles over Bryant's cheek. "You were so damn attractive, and you didn't even have a clue you were causing every cowboy who was into guys within a hundred miles to nearly break their necks trying to catch a glimpse of you.

"I'd been struggling to keep my hands off you since the first day I showed up that summer—tired from traveling and worried about what I was going to find here—and you offered to help me carry my luggage into Snake's house. I was frustrated that I couldn't have you every time I saw you out washing one of the ranch vehicles or mowing your sister's lawn, tempting me to do something I knew was wrong. I almost died that time I came across you and your cousins skinny-dipping in the back pond. When you burst up from the still waters, glistening with droplets that you shook from your hair and face while laughing, I swore I'd seen a merman or some other mythical creature designed to entrap men who should know better. You weren't old enough for all the things I wanted to do with you. Besides, I was bitter that I wasn't good enough for a Compton. I shouldn't have let that bubble over and burn you."

"Wait, what do you mean you're not good enough? You're plenty fine yourself. For a Compton or any damn person." Bryant took a step forward until he could look down into Vaughn's eyes. How dare he say shit like that about himself? "Look at everything you've done. You came for your dad even though he hadn't been a big part of your life, and you stayed for yourself. You've made something here, Vaughn. The shop. Your home. You. It's impressive."

"Now, yes." Vaughn stood straighter then. "Maybe *I* finally feel ready. For you."

Wow. Could Vaughn be serious? Bryant just needed one small double check before he launched himself onto the other guy's bed and started ripping his clothes off. "So you weren't really turned off by the fact that I didn't know what to do with a cowboy like you? A real man?"

"Nah. I would have loved to show you, to give you the answers you were looking for. But it wasn't the right thing to do." Vaughn scrunched his eyes closed. "I've never regretted doing the right thing more than I did that day...and every time I've thought about it since."

Bryant took a deep breath, then confessed, "Good, because I still don't know what I'm doing. I need you to teach me how to please a real man. I promise I'm a great student."

"I...uh...whoa." Would Vaughn turn him away again now that he knew that Bryant didn't have a single shred more experience than he had that day?

"You don't want to? I'm not going to force you, that's for fucking sure. I don't want to take anything from you that you don't want to give freely. I wouldn't have told you at all. Except I'm afraid...you're going to be disappointed." Bryant rambled, desperate to explain himself without ruining the sweet tension building between them.

Vaughn cracked up at that. He wrapped his arm around his middle and rocked until his face was as red as the prize-winning tomatoes in Vivi's garden. "I highly doubt that."

"But I'm not like the rest of the guys you've been with."

"Are you terrible at blowjobs or something?" Vaughn chuckled, as if Bryant should know how he was at going down on someone by now. Because he probably should. "What are you really trying to say, Bryant?"

"My friends at school mostly relied on social media hookup apps to find partners." He cleared his throat. "That didn't seem safe to me. After what happened...I don't trust men I don't know and I haven't met any gay guys I was into romantically. I spent a lot of time studying, not going to parties. My social life is nonexistent."

"Hang on. Are you telling me you're still a virgin?" Vaughn stiffened at that, his face going blank and unreadable.

"You know damn well I'm not." Bryant couldn't stop the shame that flooded him at the memory and the embarrassment that accompanied it, especially knowing the one man he lusted after was privy to his worst secret.

"So you've slept with other guys—at least once or twice—in the past six years, right?" Vaughn asked casually.

Bryant shook his head again. Negative.

"Are you serious? You haven't done...*anything*...since then?"

"Not unless it involved my own hands. And a few toys I got off the internet." He tried not to stumble over that confession. Like smuggling a purple mail-order Fleshlight into his dorm and hiding it under his pillow was no big deal. When one of his roommates had passed by in the hallway, he'd nearly passed out.

"Holy shit, Bryant." Vaughn didn't run this time. He reached out and drew Bryant to him. "I'm so damn sorry. And as far as I'm concerned, that day doesn't count. That wasn't sex. It was violence."

Did that mean Vaughn was about to reject him again? Tonight, of all nights, he didn't think he could stand to sleep alone. He needed a distraction from his grief—both new and old. He needed to make progress. To be sure he wasn't wasting the life not everyone had the luxury to live.

"Will you show me the difference then?" Bryant let his wildest hopes slip from his lips into the darkness before he could lock them inside.

"Yeah. I'd love to." Vaughn kept holding him close, making him forget to be awkward or afraid or sad.

Bryant hugged him back, glad for the man filling his arms. Giving him something steady to hang on to in a sea of confusion and misery. Ironically, on one of the hardest days of his life, he had found hope.

After a while, Vaughn's hands began to wander up and down his back. "Are you sure tonight is the best timing, though?"

"I want to stay." Bryant nodded.

"That's not what I said. You're not going anywhere tonight or any night you feel like this is the place you'd most like to be. You're always welcome. I'm glad I'm not alone tonight either. But...your first time should be special."

"I've waited long enough. If you're here with me, that's all I care about."

Vaughn closed his eyes for a moment, as if weighing the pros and cons. Then he opened them. The resolve there spiked Bryant's pulse. This was happening.

It wasn't a dream.

It wasn't a fantasy.

It was real life and it was going to be incredible.

7

This time, instead of retreating, Vaughn advanced. He took a step and then another until he guided Bryant backwards, toward his bedroom. "I'm going to take my time with you. Savor every moment. Every inch of you."

"That sounds good." Bryant nodded eagerly.

Vaughn chuckled. He wasn't making fun of Bryant. No, he was getting off on how much he was about to blow Bryant's mind. They both knew he would.

When the back of Bryant's knees bumped into the bed, he battled a moment of panic.

"Hey, you're not trapped. No one is forcing you to do this. If you're not into it at any time, you just say so. I'll stop. I won't be upset. I won't walk out on you. I'll stay and hold you and we'll work through it together. Unless you ask me to go. You can even have my place to yourself if you need space. I'm happy to sleep in your truck tonight. You got that?" Vaughn asked, sounding more serious than Bryant had ever heard him before. "This is all up to you. At your pace."

"Yes. Thank you."

"You don't need to thank me for being a decent human

being." Vaughn sidled closer again. This time he slid his hand beneath Bryant's shirt. He rubbed his open palm over Bryant's abs then slid it upward to his chest, soothing Bryant even as he enflamed him. Those first intimate touches made Bryant's breath stick in his lungs and his cock stand up at attention. "Would you like me to undress you?"

He nodded so hard and fast he looked like the ancient cowboy bobble-head stuck on the dash of his dad's pickup. In fact, he was about to tear his own clothes to shreds so Vaughn didn't have to waste time on getting him naked. His entire body hummed. He'd waited years for this moment and didn't want to risk anything ruining it now.

Including himself and his self-doubts.

Maybe he'd gotten soft while he was away. He didn't work the ranch every day and had eaten a few too many pizzas while he studied. Although he'd made good use of his campus's gym, it wasn't the same, really. Town life didn't seem to have impacted Vaughn, though. He could already tell Vaughn was even more cut and toned than he used to be, despite having forsaken ranch jobs. He'd grown up really, really well.

Bryant had filled out from his younger self, but he wasn't as strong as he could be. Yet.

It was time to change that.

He reached out and cupped Vaughn's stubbled jaw. Using the pad of his thumb, he brushed the other man's lips.

"That's right. I'm yours for the taking, too," Vaughn murmured, teasing Bryant's thumb with his mouth as he spoke. "Feel free to explore."

"I still wonder what it would be like to kiss you. Same as I did back then. I thought about it a lot that summer. And even more since," Bryant admitted. "The taste I had last night wasn't enough. I was in shock and it happened so fast, it felt like another fantasy. I need to do it again."

"Same here. Back then you drove me nuts with your easy

smile and quick comebacks, not to mention the way your lean muscles would put on a show while you were working. Mostly because I knew I couldn't have you. I'd hoped…after you turned eighteen…but then…"

"Enough about then." Bryant stepped closer and dropped his head so that his mouth was a hairsbreadth from Vaughn's. "Kiss me. Right now."

Vaughn didn't need to be told twice. He groaned and fused their mouths, cradling Bryant's cheeks between his hands as if trying to prove how different he could be from Bill, who'd scarred Bryant bad enough that he'd written this experience off for six whole years.

He moaned and trembled in Vaughn's grip.

It was everything he'd wished for and never gotten. Spicy, sweet, and a little bit desperate.

Patiently, Vaughn showed him how to make it even better with swirls of his tongue, the hint of teeth, and a seductive rhythm they naturally fell into as they discovered how well they meshed. Bryant didn't have anything to compare it to, but he figured it was as good as he suspected when Vaughn drew back, panting, to rest his forehead on Bryant's.

He stared into Bryant's eyes just long enough to catch his breath and whisper, "Damn," before going back for seconds. Instead of ramping up their exchange, Vaughn seemed content to dwell. He pressed Bryant's shoulders, though, urging him to sink onto the bed if he chose.

It wasn't a shove. He wasn't demanding it.

It was a suggestion.

One Bryant gladly took. He wanted to settle in and savor these moments. The ones where his eyes were opened to the magnitude of pleasure he could find with the perfect partner. He lay down and Vaughn followed, never breaking their contact. When Bryant tried to settle onto his back, Vaughn rolled him to his side instead. Probably so that he wasn't fully on top of Bryant.

While part of him appreciated not feeling pinned down, most of him regretted the loss of Vaughn's comforting heat and weight on top of him. Sometime when he was able to actually form words, he'd tell Vaughn that he didn't mind the pressure.

For now, he was content to make out with Vaughn, mimicking the motions he made with his mouth. His toes curled when he made Vaughn moan. To know he could affect his partner, even as skilled as he was, made Bryant feel like less of a complete failure.

He was on euphoria overload. He dropped his head back to gasp for air and Vaughn slowly descended, giving him ample time to object, which he definitely didn't do. Vaughn began to spread his kisses over Bryant's exposed neck, licking and sucking places Bryant never knew could be so fucking sensitive. He squirmed on Vaughn's bed.

Oh God, he was in Vaughn's *bed*.

That thought alone had his cock throbbing in his jeans. He groaned. Going slow like this was its own form of delicious torture. One he didn't mind in the least.

When his eyelids drifted open, he saw Vaughn tensed with desires of his own. Was Bryant being selfish? Making the other guy wait when he needed more?

"Is this okay? For you?" Bryant asked.

"Fucking incredible," Vaughn murmured, as if in awe. "Not sure if I've ever really taken the time to get this amped up before rushing to the finish line. It's different with you. New and amazing. I could do this all night."

It made something deep inside Bryant blossom to know Vaughn was exploring uncharted territory just like him. He relaxed and gave himself permission to ask for more. "You said you were going to undress me. Do it, please. I want to feel your skin on mine while we kiss."

Vaughn hesitated, taking several deep breaths. "You're going to kill me. If my heart explodes and I croak in bed, just tell everyone I went out the happiest I've ever been."

"Do you really mean that?" Bryant traced Vaughn's swollen lower lip with the tip of one finger.

"I'm probably not *actually* going to die. It just feels like it. More like I already have and I'm in heaven." Vaughn winked.

Bryant laughed. "Not that. I mean, does this really make you happy?"

"Yeah. It's kind of weird. I feel more than horny in bed. I feel...like it's been too long since I was kissing you because I want to share more of this sensation with you."

How could he resist that? Bryant reached out and drew Vaughn close again. "Multitask then. Kiss me but take my clothes off, too. Can you do that?"

"I think so." Vaughn flashed a wicked grin before he sealed their mouths. His fingers deftly unbuttoned Bryant's shirt. Never hurrying. He slipped each button through the hole, then trailed his fingers along the bare skin he exposed before working on the next.

Why the fuck did this shirt need so many buttons anyway? Bryant arched, trying to press his chest closer to Vaughn. When he'd finally finished, Vaughn clasped Bryant's hands in his. Their fingers entwined for a while even as their legs scissored and their mouths kept devouring each other. Only when Bryant made a tortured sound low in his throat did Vaughn place Bryant's hands at the top of his shirt.

Bryant couldn't say he was as suave as Vaughn. He fumbled, then resorted to tugging a few of the buttons off, but eventually he freed Vaughn's torso. He couldn't stop himself from kneading the muscles there as they stared into each other's eyes, always kissing.

They rolled around on the bed, wrestling each other's shirts off without interrupting their make-out session. They tumbled over each other, tugging and straining, rubbing against each other in the most delicious foreplay imaginable.

When Bryant ended up straddling Vaughn, he broke the kiss, just for a moment, to get a good look at his partner. "Damn, you're gorgeous."

He raked his fingers down Vaughn's body from his collarbones, over his chest and tight nipples, along the valley of his ripped abdomen to the trail of hair that disappeared into his waistband. He rocked his hips, grinding their denim-covered cocks together.

Thank god for the thick material, or Bryant would definitely have lost it by now. His balls were tight and close to his body, drawn up at the thought of how this would end.

He never wanted it to end.

"You are, too." Vaughn echoed his thoughts and his gestures, running his hands over Bryant's arms, chest, and finally down to his ass. He squeezed hard and used the grip to guide Bryant, keeping him rubbing their hard-ons together through their pants. "Do you want to show me your cock? Let me suck it?"

"Son of a bitch." Bryant threw his head back and clenched his jaw. He damn near came in his pants at the thought alone.

"Is that a yes?" Vaughn asked, his fingers hovering over the button on Bryant's fly.

"Hell yes. But..." Bryant swallowed hard.

"But what?"

"I don't even know if you'll get it all the way in your mouth before I come. I'm on the edge. Just from making out with you." He turned his head to the side, feeling his cheeks heat.

"Hey, you're doing better than I did. My first time, I shot the second I rode the guy's thigh while making out with him." Vaughn grinned. "Don't worry. If you want to come, come. It'll take the edge off. I'll get you hard again eventually. There's no hurry tonight."

Bryant knew right then that more than his virginity was at stake. He wanted to give himself to Vaughn. His heart included. A dangerous proposition. So he pretended to himself that things weren't so serious. That it was just a hookup. No big deal.

Then he nodded. "Please. I'd love to know what it feels like to have someone suck my cock."

From the bragging his cousins did, he knew it was a highlight of their sex lives. Bryant wanted to be in on the secret. Even if it meant craving something he couldn't have all the time.

Vaughn licked his lips, then popped the button on Bryant's fly before unzipping it carefully. He wrapped his fingers in the waistband of Bryant's jeans and walked them down his hips and thighs. When Vaughn ran out of room, his fists at his sides and the jeans strangling Bryant's knees, Bryant rolled to the side, landing on his back. Vaughn came over him and finished the job, peeling the denim down and off Bryant's socked feet before getting rid of those and his underwear, too.

Then he was naked. Bared to Vaughn's hungry gaze. Vaughn scanned him from head to toe, taking special note of his cock, which had never been as long or hard as it was in that moment. It lay heavy on his belly, leaking precome onto his abs. "Damn, Bryant. You're impressive."

"Come on, I'm not that naïve. I've watched a lot of porn. If anything, I'm average."

Vaughn grinned. "Average guys don't star in porn."

"Oh." Why hadn't he considered that? Right then, reasoning was beyond him. There were other things more important. "Can I see you, too?"

"In a minute," Vaughn said. "I want to touch you. Is that okay?"

Bryant didn't hesitate. He reached out and tugged Vaughn's hand straight to his cock. When the other man fisted his dick, a primitive howl flew from Bryant's throat. He saw stars as Vaughn adjusted his grip before massaging his shaft with ripples of his fingers. Jesus. He'd imagined it would be great, but he'd had no idea it would be so much more intense than jerking off when someone else touched him.

Someone he desired. Someone who respected him and only cared about bringing *him* pleasure.

God, he'd been so stupid.

He refused to think about that now, while Vaughn nearly made his eyes roll so far back inside his skull that he read equations from his research, which were imprinted on his neocortex. Bryant lifted his hips, shoving his cock deeper into Vaughn's grasp.

"Does that feel good?" Vaughn asked.

"Shit, yes," he growled.

"Do you like it more like this..." Vaughn left his hand looser and jacked the tip a few times. "Or like this...?" Then he tightened his grip and made full-length strokes with his fist.

When the side of his hand bumped Bryant's balls, he couldn't decide. "Both. I like both."

Vaughn chuckled. "It's so fun to experiment with you like this. Don't worry. I know something you'll like even better than either of those."

"Not sure that's possible." Bryant dug his toes into Vaughn's comforter to keep from flying into space. He wasn't a rocket scientist, but he was pretty sure they generated enough energy between them to shoot him into orbit.

Without bothering to argue, Vaughn sank between Bryant's legs and cupped his balls in his palm. He rolled them lightly while still jerking Bryant off. And just when Bryant thought he might come before he felt Vaughn's mouth on him, the other guy leaned in and licked around the head of his dick while his hand kept up its magic.

"Vaughn!" He wasn't sure if he was calling out for the other guy to stop or to do more. All he knew was that his focus was lasered in on the places where they intersected and the things Vaughn was capable of doing to him.

"I'm right here, Bryant. I've got you," he whispered. "Remember, you're safe with me. It's okay to let go. I want you come. For me. Whenever you're ready."

Bryant looked at Vaughn then, and saw him open his mouth as he approached, slowly. Waiting for affirmation that it was okay to proceed.

"Please," was the only thing Bryant could say.

The humid suction that enveloped his cock in the next moment shocked him in the best of ways. He never imagined it could be like this. Damn, his cousins had been holding back. Their rave reviews still hadn't done this justice. The pressure of Vaughn sucking, interrupted by light laps of his tongue, kept Bryant on the edge of rapture longer than he thought he would make it.

He tensed but held there, suspended in euphoria, as Vaughn slid down his shaft, taking it all in his mouth. When Bryant's cock bumped his soft, hot flesh, the ex-cowboy did something with his jaw and welcomed Bryant into his throat.

He swallowed around the entire length of Bryant's hard-on, proving that even if Bryant was bigger than normal, it wasn't a problem for his partner. As the pressure increased, Vaughn flicked the pad of his thumb up the center line of Bryant's sac. He used his tongue to lave the underside of Bryant's cock.

But when he hummed, like Bryant's erection was the most delicious thing he'd ever put in his mouth...that's what got Bryant. He tensed, his eyes flying wide open as he peered down at Vaughn.

The guy smiled around Bryant and nodded, letting him know it was fine to come in his mouth.

So he did.

His balls tensed impossibly, then exploded as he shot jet

after jet straight down Vaughn's throat. The guy drank it all, drawing more and more pleasure from Bryant. He'd never been caught in the throes of an orgasm for so long. Part of his scientific mind wondered just how long a single climax could last as his body continued to spasm. Hard.

But not very much of it. The majority of his being was dedicated to wringing every drop of rapture from the generosity of his lover. *Lover.* He couldn't believe that's what Vaughn was to him now. That thought alone added another several pulses to Bryant's epic release.

And when Vaughn had drunk him dry, Bryant collapsed, exhausted and drained onto the guy's pillows. Holy fuck. Was that normal, what he'd just experienced? "Vaughn."

"Damn, Bryant. I thought you were going to drown me there for a second. You've been saving that up for a long fucking time." He wiped his mouth on the back of his hand then crawled up to lie beside Bryant, cradling him against his chest.

When Bryant still couldn't respond, Vaughn ran his fingers through Bryant's hair. "You okay?"

"Mmm," he managed to purr. It was a little while later, when enough of his mind began to function properly, that he noticed Vaughn's raging hard-on, which was leaving an impression on his hip. When he reached for it, Vaughn dodged.

"You don't have to do that." He kissed Bryant's forehead. "Just savor the afterglow."

"I think I'll enjoy the hell out of making you feel half as good as I do right now." He reached for Vaughn's cock again. This time the other guy didn't stop him. Bryant rubbed it through Vaughn's jeans for a minute before Vaughn caved and shoved them off, flinging his pants somewhere in the distance. "Just tell me what to do. What *you* like, since you already know."

"You're sure?"

"Hell yes." Bryant extended his hand again, this time not

stopping until he clutched Vaughn's cock. He studied the feel of it, silky yet hard, hot and smooth, in his fingers. He rubbed it artlessly, until he realized it wasn't so different from jacking himself.

So he did what he liked, hoping that was good enough for Vaughn.

When his partner moaned and kissed the shit out of him, he figured it didn't suck too bad.

Eventually, Vaughn came up for air. He stared down at Bryant, his eyes practically glowing in the lamplight. "Use your other hand on yourself. Get yourself hard again for me."

That wasn't going to be a problem.

But Bryant did as he was told. He hissed at the first touch of his palm on his shaft.

"Keep it there. Good. Just like that." Vaughn growled. "Don't stop stroking us, okay? Can you do that for me?"

"Uh huh." Bryant concentrated on keeping the pace steady, not rushing and pushing them further than they could resist, but refusing to falter either.

"I'm going to make it even better for you. Is it okay if I play with your ass?" Vaughn nuzzled Bryant's neck then bit his shoulder lightly as he waited for a response. He didn't press the issue or move any closer to his intended target until Bryant thought about the question hard and answered.

"Yeah."

"If you don't like it, tell me to stop. That's fine. This is all about you and figuring out what you like, remember?" Vaughn kissed the place he'd nipped, then lifted his head to stare into Bryant's eyes and make sure they were on the same page.

Bryant nodded enthusiastically.

Vaughn smiled and reached for the table beside his bed. He didn't roll away so far that Bryant had to relinquish his grasp on Vaughn's cock, for which he was grateful. Holding the proof of Vaughn's arousal in his fist helped him ignore the parts of himself that were insisting he couldn't possibly do anything for a man used to sleeping with guys who could handle a stud like him in bed.

His grip must have tightened involuntarily.

Vaughn moaned, then chuckled. "I'm coming right back, promise."

Bryant groaned, self-conscious about how much he needed more of Vaughn. A lot more.

He rubbed their cocks in unison, giving them both the same pleasure, which was amplified by the knowledge that Vaughn was feeling what he was. They were in this together. And if Vaughn got off on whatever he was about to do, Bryant couldn't wait for him to start.

Vaughn found whatever he was looking for and returned to Bryant's side. He knelt between Bryant's legs for a moment, aligning their shafts so they pressed together. Bryant wrapped his hands around them both and pumped them simultaneously. Even their balls rested against each other. They were a perfect match.

"Damn, Bryant." Vaughn leaned in to kiss Bryant for a bit more. "That feels amazing, but I want to show you more. How good it can be."

"Yes." Bryant wanted that, too. He didn't want to waste this chance in case it was the only one he ever got to explore with the partner of his dreams.

Vaughn resettled himself at Bryant's side, his cock jutting out over Bryant's hip. Bryant never let go, never stopped playing with his new favorite toy while also caressing his own hard-on.

When Vaughn nudged his thigh—the one not trapped beneath the leg Vaughn threw over the one closest to him— Bryant instinctively spread his legs. He bent his knee and planted his foot on the mattress, leaving himself open to whatever Vaughn wanted to show him.

His heartbeat quickened.

"You're fine, Bryant," Vaughn murmured in his ear. "You're here with me and only me. Don't think about the past. Just concentrate on now and how this feels. We can stop at any time. Okay?"

Bryant nodded.

A moment later, he heard squishy sounds as Vaughn slathered his fingers in lube. "This might be cool at first, but trust me, it's going to heat up fast."

Bryant gulped. He let his knee drop outward, making more room for Vaughn's advancing hand.

When the tip of one greased finger nudged his ass, Bryant yelped.

Vaughn chuckled. "I told you."

Except it wasn't the cold that had spooked him, it was the fact that he was letting someone do this to him again, after hiding from his desires for so long.

Before he could explain, Vaughn carefully inserted the tip of his finger. When it didn't burn or tear, Bryant relaxed. That only made it easier for Vaughn to prod deeper. He moved his finger in a circle, massaging nerve endings Bryant hadn't known existed. But now that he did, he wanted more.

A lot more.

Vaughn smiled down at him. "Good?"

"Mmm." He lifted his hips, driving Vaughn's hand deeper.

So the other man responded by adding a second digit. He spread them within Bryant, opening him farther, making him crave more. This went on for what seemed like hours. Every time Bryant adjusted to the pleasure and pressure, Vaughn would increase it until Bryant didn't know how he could stand anymore. Not because it hurt, but because it flooded him with bliss.

After a while, he realized that although he could easily come with Vaughn's fingers teasing his hole and the sensitive places within him, he didn't want to. He craved more of his lover.

"Vaughn, fuck me. Please." Bryant squirmed, impaled on Vaughn's fingers, which were wonderful, though not nearly enough.

Instead of plunging inside him, Vaughn hesitated. "I'm not sure you're ready. Why don't we take it slow tonight?"

"I'm telling you....I'm fucking ready. This is what I want. You. Inside me. Right now."

Vaughn's face flushed. His eyes dilated and he crushed his mouth to Bryant's for a few moments. Then he lifted off and said, "I promised you anything you asked for. As long as you're sure."

"Stop talking and start fucking." Bryant had no idea where this side of him came from, but he kind of liked it. All of the careful consideration he usually relied on as a crutch to keep from making terrible decisions flew out the window. He acted on instinct. Pure, raw, feelings.

Vaughn grinned. "I like it when you're bossy."

"Then why aren't you buried balls-deep yet?"

Vaughn pinched Bryant's nipple playfully. "Hang on. Let me grab a condom."

"You don't need to. I'm clean if you are." Bryant shrugged.

"No. I'm going to protect you. Like I should have done before. Some other time, when you're thinking straight, you can make that call. Not tonight." Vaughn wouldn't budge on that point.

Though he was a little disappointed he wouldn't have Vaughn inside him bare, Bryant appreciated his concern. It reassured him that this was the right time and the right person and that it was okay to give in to the overwhelming emotions swamping him.

Vaughn retrieved and donned a condom before slathering himself in more lube. He added another dab to Bryant's ass as well before fitting the tip against Bryant's hole. Even that tiny contact sent shockwaves through Bryant's body.

It was real. This was happening.

He braced himself for the agony he'd felt that day in the barn, sure Vaughn's pleasure was worth the sacrifice.

Vaughn leaned down and distracted Bryant with a tender kiss that stole his breath. It relaxed him, allowing the increasing insistence of Vaughn's cock to push it the barest bit inside Bryant's ass. It surprised him that it didn't hurt. In fact, he wanted more.

He put his hands on Vaughn's hips and tried to pull him closer, deeper, but Vaughn resisted. "Don't rush me. I'm going to give you all of me. Just not all at once. That's nonnegotiable. I refuse to hurt you."

Though he didn't say it, they both knew he meant...like Bryant's attacker had.

Overwhelming affection snuck in beside the arousal threatening to drown Bryant. He slid his hands higher, up Vaughn's back, until he could hug him. He squeezed tight and hoped Vaughn knew how much this meant.

Vaughn nibbled on his lower lip, then resumed his rocking, letting Bryant adjust to the widening head of his cock and how it reopened his ass like his fingers had earlier. Lost in the fluid glides of Vaughn's tongue over his own, Bryant didn't notice Vaughn's cock had slid fully into his ass until Vaughn paused to draw a deep, shaky breath.

The amount of control and stamina he had impressed Bryant.

The fact that he used his prowess to bring Bryant only pleasure—and tons of it—blew his mind.

He reached between them to fist his cock, in desperate need of contact there.

"Let me get that for you." Vaughn replaced Bryant's hand with his own. "I'm going to come so hard and deep in you,

Bryant. You can watch what you do to me. But not before you're taken care of. You're going to shoot first. I want to feel your come splattering on my chest and abs. I need to know you like this—that you're getting off on it—before I can do the same."

"Jesus, Vaughn. I love it." He almost slipped up and said that he loved Vaughn, but even he knew that would be a rookie mistake. Just because he was giving the man his virginity didn't mean Vaughn wanted more of him than that.

Then the ability to form coherent thoughts dissolved. Vaughn took up where Bryant had left off, stroking his cock even as he began to penetrate farther into Bryant's ass. There wasn't a single flicker of discomfort, and certainly no agony. It was all ecstasy as Vaughn filled him inch by inch. Bryant spread and lifted his legs, giving Vaughn room to work.

"Yes, that's right," Vaughn coached. "Let me in."

Vaughn rocked his hips, working himself deeper until his balls tapped Bryant's ass. Bryant looked down and saw their bodies pressed together. He had all of Vaughn within him. He shivered, his muscles tightening involuntarily. He clenched his ass around Vaughn's cock, making them both groan.

"Are you okay?" Vaughn asked, his voice rough though calm.

"Amazing."

"Yes, you are." Vaughn kissed him more, his hand squeezing Bryant's cock when it didn't have space to rub the full length of his shaft. While they made out, he began to withdraw, every bit as slowly as he'd impaled Bryant.

Bryant made a strangled noise. He didn't want Vaughn to go.

"Shhh." The other man kissed his forehead, then straightened some. "I'm coming right back."

True to his word, he reversed his motion, stroking Bryant from the inside with long, slow plunges. Meanwhile, his fist mimicked the path of his cock. He rubbed Bryant in time with his fucking, making him imagine what it would be like to be inside Vaughn instead.

Bryant clenched his jaw as a squirt of precome pulsed from the tip of his cock, coating Vaughn's knuckles. Vaughn didn't hesitate—he lifted his hand to his mouth and licked it off as if it were a delicacy.

The next time he slid into Bryant, he was a little less careful, a little less slow.

Bryant loved it and craved more. "Harder. Faster. Please."

He knew he couldn't last forever, despite having come so hard earlier. He needed to do it again and he had a feeling that what he thought could never be topped would be a mere shadow of the rapture Vaughn was about to unleash within him.

Without speaking, Vaughn listened. He ramped up the pace and force of his fucking. In addition to the bolts of ecstasy shooting up Bryant's spine from his ass, the masterful stroking of his cock had him writhing beneath Vaughn in short order.

Vaughn stared into his eyes, making sure he was okay. That he was loving every second of their encounter. And he was.

In fact, he loved it a little too much.

"Vaughn!" he cried, trying to keep himself from coming too soon and putting an end to the most glorious thing he'd ever felt.

"Oh no. Don't hold back." Vaughn leaned in and bit Bryant's shoulder lightly. "Feel what I'm doing to you. What you do to me. By being so damn sexy and cute and fun and smart. This is all for you. Because of you. Tonight, no one else would do. It had to be you."

That was the most arousing thing Vaughn had done to him yet. Make him feel like he was special. Like this meant something. Like he'd been right to wait so damn long for the perfect partner.

There was no way he could resist that.

Bryant's ass clamped around Vaughn's cock. He felt every ridge of the other man's shaft as it plowed into him over and over relentlessly. He shuddered, then stared directly into Vaughn's eyes as he lost control completely.

"That's right. Come, Bryant. Come hard. Shoot all over me. Show me how much you love my cock in your ass. Fucking you. *Finally* fucking you." Vaughn seemed lost in his own euphoria. He rambled as he drilled into Bryant, harder and faster, pushing him into climax.

Bryant pounded the mattress with his fists, shook his head on the pillow, and then roared as seed blasted from his cock. Vaughn didn't stop pumping his shaft or filling his ass. But he aimed Bryant's dick at himself and took the first blast of seed directly on his chest. He twitched as if it seared him, then went into a frenzy, fucking Bryant with a flurry of short, fast jabs that tapped his prostate over and over while he unloaded on Vaughn.

Seeing his own come glazing the other man's abdomen and chest extended Bryant's pleasure. And apparently, it ramped up Vaughn's. He grunted, then plunged deep, locking them together. He shouted Bryant's name and let him see how awed he was as he too began to climax.

Bryant brought his arms up to hold Vaughn close as he flooded the condom he'd insisted on wearing. Next time, Bryant promised himself he'd take the proof of Vaughn's enjoyment and hold it deep within him. Absorbing it as if it was his own.

Because it was. Seeing the shock, rapture, and disbelief in Vaughn's eyes made Bryant's cock twitch with aftershocks. The intensity of the exchange caught him completely off guard. No matter what happened from this point on, he felt like part of him would belong to Vaughn for the rest of their lives.

He'd given the other man his virginity, but he'd gotten so much more in return.

This was what he'd always been missing.

And now he'd found it again.

Thanks to Vaughn.

Bryant melted into the plush bed, every ounce of sadness, grief, fear, and regret erased from his soul for that moment. He lay in a daze as Vaughn cared for him. Cleaning him, then crawling into bed to embrace him, crooning praise and who knew what else, kissing him gently as they came back down from the enormous high they'd reached together.

It was almost as good as the sex, the intimacy they wove afterward.

Bryant fought sleep for as long as he could, soaking in the comfort and closeness of their bond. Eventually he couldn't resist and fell into a deep, dreamless slumber, with Vaughn wrapped protectively around him.

8

———

Afaint scratching noise roused Bryant from his deep sleep. Sure, he'd been deprived after his marathon drive home from college and a restless night following the bonfire, but that didn't account for how hard he'd crashed after making love with Vaughn.

From the light already sneaking in around the edges of the room-darkening shades Vaughn must use since he usually worked nights, Bryant figured his dad and the rest of the ranch had already been up and working for hours. Damn.

He pushed up onto his elbows, reluctant to leave the oasis Vaughn had made for them and return to the real world. He squinted at Vaughn, who lounged stretched out alongside him, something white and rectangular balanced on one knee. Bryant blinked and scrubbed his eyes with the back of his knuckles. "What are you doing?"

"Shit, sorry. I didn't mean to wake you." Vaughn paused whatever he was up to, a pencil clutched in his hand. The tip hovered over an old-fashioned notebook. The paper kind, not the electronic sort everyone else Bryant knew used these days.

91

"Are you drawing? Can I see?" Curiosity piqued, he levered himself higher and craned his neck.

Vaughn tipped his pad away from Bryant. "It's nothing important. Just doodling."

"I let you fuck me stupid. The least you could do is trust me enough to show me your art. You're really great at it, you know. I've seen all the tattoos you've given Austin and Sterling. They love them. Makes me sort of wish I had something I wanted permanently on *my* skin."

"Really?" Vaughn raised his brows. "Okay then. What do you think about this?"

He showed Bryant what he'd been sketching.

It was him. Lying naked in Vaughn's bed. Except in the drawing, he was covered with ink. Most notably, a full chest piece.

The details were hazy, but there was a compass, the silhouette of a cowboy that even pre-coffee screamed Jake, and water. The entire thing was surrounded by a background of splashes that made it look as if someone had dropped it into a puddle or maybe the pond where Vaughn had stumbled across him skinny dipping that summer so long ago. There was a particularly smudgy spot at the center where it looked like Vaughn had erased something from his work in progress.

Bryant grinned. Seeing himself through Vaughn's eyes boosted his ego. He looked more like the cowboy he'd been raised to be instead of the repressed nerd he'd thought of himself as for too long. "Well, damn. I look pretty fucking hot tatted up."

"Uh huh." Vaughn nodded, his eyes turning hungry again.

"What's that?" Bryant asked as he pointed to the indistinct section of the sketch.

Vaughn shook his head. "Nothing, yet."

"What could it be?" It was fascinating to behold the potential Vaughn saw in him come to life. To imagine that he might become that self-assured, sinfully sexy man, who indulged in a wild affair and gave as good as he got if they spent too many more nights like this one together.

"I guess that's up to you." Vaughn refused to meet his stare. "It's just a dumb sketch."

Funny, it felt more like a vision to Bryant. A glimpse of a very promising future where he became the man he'd always wanted to be. A real Compton. "Could I have it?"

Vaughn hesitated, as if he wanted to keep it. Then he smiled. "Sure. I'll even sign it for you."

He scribbled his signature at the bottom along with 1/2.

"What's the 1/2 for?" Bryant wondered.

"One of two. I'm going to draw myself a copy." He grinned. "I want to remember this night forever. I hope you don't mind me keeping a souvenir. I promise I don't do this with every guy I sleep with. I don't hoard pictures of my conquests. It's just you. This...meant something to me."

Bryant knew it was sappy, but he squirmed a little inside anyway. To know that he could have this—a man who was a powerhouse alpha in bed and still romantic. That he could learn to stand just as strong. It was everything he'd ever dreamed of. Wished for.

He reached up and tugged Vaughn's shoulders toward him some. Not enough so that they ended up tangled together on the sheets, though he wished he had time for that. Just a bit, so that he could kiss Vaughn, and remind them both of how they'd spent so much of last night.

"I take it that means it's okay?" Vaughn made sure not to violate Bryant, which only made him second-guess the building urge he had to get up and get dressed.

"Of course. Hopefully you can do it from memory, though. I've got to go home. I need to talk to my dad about sponsoring my thesis project for school." Tension began to seep back into his muscles, knotting them.

Vaughn rubbed his back, easing it again. "Hey, you know he'll do it. Sam and your uncles would do anything for you. I think that's why Jake never told them about what happened. He was afraid they'd get themselves in trouble by going after that prick and tearing him apart."

"Probably true." Bryant sighed. "But I want my dad to agree because it's a sound investment for the ranch, not because he's my dad. I've taken enough. I need to give something back. But it's a lot of money. What if it doesn't work like I think—"

"Hey." Vaughn shook him a little then. "You've got this. You don't give yourself enough credit. You're better than you think you are. Especially at blowjobs, though you're welcome to practice on me anytime if you're still not sure about that."

Bryant snorted a laugh. "Thanks."

Vaughn kissed him quickly, stopping before either of them could get sidetracked. "I guess I better clean up the shop, send appointment reminders, put in the supply order, and get ready for reopening this afternoon. My schedule is packed since I cancelled appointments yesterday and so many people want Jake memorials."

"They do? That's amazing." Bryant considered whether or not he should do something similar. Listening to Austin's ideas for his own design the night before had sparked something in Bryant. Not to mention Vaughn's drawings. He'd have to think about it. "Well, I better let you get to it then."

Had he taken too much of Vaughn's time? And when he left, was Vaughn expecting him to come back...tonight or ever?

As if he could sense Bryant's hesitation, Vaughn asked softly, "When can I see you again?"

"I'm not sure. I'm going to be ridiculously busy trying to get this thing built and functional in time to finish my thesis by the deadline."

"When is that, exactly?" Vaughn wondered.

"A month from yesterday. The theoretical part of my paper

took a lot longer than anticipated to complete and get approved." Bryant winced as he sat up and flung his legs over the edge of the bed. There really wasn't any time to waste.

Vaughn whistled. "That's not very long. Do you need an assistant? I don't have to work until the evening. I could help out with the grunt work. Come out there early, before the days get too hot. I could probably put in five or six hours each morning for as long as you need me."

Bryant wasn't about to turn down either a hand or the chance to spend more time with Vaughn. "That would be great. You know, *if* my dad agrees."

"Go on, then." Vaughn slapped Bryant's ass and turned him toward the door. "You're not going to feel better until you hash it out with him."

"I'm not going to feel better until I provide substantial hydrological resources for Compass Ranch and earn my doctoral degree."

"Overachiever." Vaughn grinned. "I can't wait to call you Dr. Compton. That will be something."

It set him on fire that Vaughn was so proud of him and his achievements. So certain that Bryant had it in him to see this through. It did a lot to bolster his confidence as he got dressed, kissed Vaughn goodbye, then climbed into his truck, and headed home.

When he took one final glance in his rearview mirror and saw Vaughn standing out on his balcony, watching him go, he had to blink away the moisture in his eyes.

He looked skyward and whispered, "Thanks, Jake. You were right. As always."

9

———

"Dad, can I talk to you about something?" Bryant thought back to Jake's advice as he hovered on the threshold to his father's office, where Sam managed the ranch and its financials.

He was ready to make a significant contribution to Compass Ranch. He just needed his father to believe he was capable of it. To trust him and take a chance. Then be able to deliver on the promises he made to Jake, his dad, the thesis board, and himself.

"Hey, Bryant." Sam waved him inside and toward a chair. "Of course. Sorry I haven't spent more time catching up. This past week… It's been rough."

Bryant had heard some rumors. About his mother, father, Jake, and the special relationship they'd had, especially when she was—hell, about the age he was now. Things he didn't honestly understand or want to know all the details about. Based on the shred of evidence Jake had given him in their final phone conversation, the gossip likely held some truth. His parents seemed to be mourning Jake harder than even the Compass Boys, who'd always thought of him as their surrogate grandfather, seeing as JD had passed away before they were born.

"I can come back some other time." He shifted from one boot to another. It felt odd to be wearing them again. He'd gotten used to the dress shoes he'd donned in his lab. Not that different from his father, he supposed, who'd gone to New York City for a time to work as some kind of financial guru before he'd returned to Compass Ranch when JD had gotten cancer.

In that way, they were a lot alike. Neither had the desire to work the land the way Uncle Silas or Uncle Seth did. That didn't mean his father wasn't crucial to the ranch's success. It also meant Bryant had some chance to make an equal impact in his own way...if he stood up for himself now and asked for what he needed in order to prove his worth.

"Actually, no. Dad, I take it back." Bryant tucked his hands in his pockets. He rocked on his heels yet held his ground. "I need to talk to you now."

"It must be serious." His dad cocked his head sideways, sort of like a confused dog. "I've never seen you quite like this."

Bryant nodded.

Sam smiled. "I like it."

"You might not when you hear what I'm thinking." Bryant stepped closer and leaned his hip against his father's desk. "It's like this: I have to do a final project. Something to give my thesis some merit. I have to implement a practical application that demonstrates the viability of my design developments."

"Anything you need for school, you know we're behind you." Sam smiled. "We're proud of you, *Dr. Compton*."

Bryant wished people would stop calling him that until it was official. It felt like they might jinx it or something. Besides, he hadn't earned the honor quite yet.

"If this goes right, I'll deserve that." He didn't want to hide behind his degree, though. This was about more than an assignment. "It's not just school I'm talking about. I feel like I can do something for the ranch. Something major. I'd talked about my ideas some with Jake. He agreed they would be a good fit for our operations."

Now he wasn't there to help him pitch his dad on a major outlay.

So Bryant would have to do it for them both.

"He might not have had three degrees." Sam crossed his arms, poking fun at himself and his own MBA every bit as much as Bryant's higher education. "But he was a smart man. One of the most intuitive I've ever met. Let's hear it. If he approved, I'm sure I'll agree."

"It hinges on recapturing evapotranspiration and channeling those resources. Attacking our consumption rates through an intelligent irrigation system while increasing the reserves on the ranch. There's a special polymer I can infuse in the soil. It will retain up to four hundred percent more moisture than untreated soil. In addition, we can add reserve tanks and modify the feed types we're growing. With these and other adjustments, plus the addition of catchment and retention systems, we can expect to drop our reliance on fresh rainwater to seventeen percent of today's requirements."

"Son, I'm not going to pretend I understand seventeen percent of what you're saying right now, except I think you're telling me that we'd be able to survive an epic drought with the changes you want to make. Is that right?" His dad's face grew serious.

Bryant nodded. "Yes. Even with the crazy weather patterns and climate change shifts we've been seeing, we could be insulated from most of those seasonal variations. I project that once everything is online and at capacity, we could sustain Compass Ranch's average water usage for two full years, potentially longer."

"Well, shit. That would be...incredible." Sam rubbed his hand over his face. "So how much is all this going to cost us?"

"I could do a tiny mockup that would generate enough evidence to finish my project for about seven grand. But if you want me to do it right, to actually implement my designs...to go all in, we'd be looking at closer to a hundred thousand dollars."

Sam spun around in his chair at that. He whistled as he stared out at the ranch behind them. "That's a lot of money, son. At any time, but especially now. We've got a lot tied up in Seth's new line and allocated for an upgraded rig for Austin. It's..."

Bryant tried to rein in his disappointment. There would always be another shot later. "I understand."

"No, I don't think you do." Sam rotated back to stare at Bryant. "I need a couple of days to make some calls, but you're going to have that cash. Jake believed in you, and so do I. Don't ever doubt it."

Bryant whipped around and stared at the wall until his eyes stopped stinging dangerously. "Thank you."

"No, Bryant. Thank *you*. For making our home a better place."

"It's not done yet. And...Dad, it's an experiment. It might not work. I could fail. Bad."

"Do you believe you've got something?" Sam asked.

Bryant nodded. "I've done the calculations a million times. It should work."

"Then it will." Sam shrugged as if it were already a foregone conclusion.

"I can't control the weather, though." Bryant wanted to make absolutely sure his dad understood the risk they were taking. "I can build the system. Lay the foundation. But if it doesn't rain enough, it won't be up to full capacity. Ideally, this should have been finished months ago. We've missed almost the entire spring already..."

"Don't do that, Bryant." Sam leveled a stern look he'd reserved for times like when he, Austin, Doug, and James had accidentally burned down one of the ranch's sheds when they were kids.

He took a step back. "What did I do?"

"Doubted yourself." Sam leaned forward then. "You're bright as fuck. And a good kid. I wish you'd see what the rest of us do when we look at you."

Bryant's stare inadvertently slid to the mirror on the wall beside his father's desk. It surprised him, seeing them both reflected there, how alike they were. As he aged, he was starting to look more and more like a Compton. But he'd never quite felt like one inside.

Because he was gay? Maybe, though his family had been very accepting when they'd realized he was into guys. Just like his project, however, it had been a theoretical exercise. He'd never brought a guy around, or even been with one, not since that day in the barn.

He didn't even want to think about that in his dad's office in case the guy could read his mind or something. Jake had taken that secret to his grave. The only person around who knew about it now was Vaughn.

Vaughn.

Bryant thought of the night before and the subtle ache in his muscles today. What would his family say if they knew how he'd spent the hours after Jake's funeral? He didn't think it was disrespectful to his hero. After all, Jake had told him he should have hooked up with Vaughn.

Hopefully it wasn't too late to take his advice.

"Anything else you want to talk about? Your sister mentioned you didn't come home last night. She was worried until I told her about Vaughn's truck parked in the yard." Sam rocked back and put his boots on his desk, his legs crossed at the ankles. "I know you boys confided in Jake and relied on his advice, but I hope you never forget that I'm here for you. Me and your uncles. Your mom and your aunts. You can talk to any of us at any time."

Yeah. Right. Bryant wasn't about to be sharing the intimate details of his love life with his father.

But maybe just one thing... "Are you disappointed that I'm gay?"

Sam laughed so hard he started coughing. Until he realized Bryant was serious. "What would ever make you wonder about that? I don't care who you're attracted to. As long as they're of age and you treat each other with respect, I'll be glad when you find someone to love. Seriously, Bryant, have you spent more than one moment worrying about that? Ever?"

He nodded slowly. "It's not easy growing up around all of you dominant guys. Uncle Silas, Uncle Seth, you, Uncle Sawyer, you're enough to give a guy a complex."

"What about Uncle Colby?" Sam shrugged.

"What about him?" He was just as fierce as the rest. Another Compton man with brass balls bigger than Bryant would ever have. "Jake said something about him too. That I should talk to him sometime."

"See, you should listen to your elders. I mean, you remind me a lot of him when he was your age." His dad tapped his chin. "I guess he's changed some over time, but he was always happy to let Silas take the lead. Nothing wrong with that. He also kept your uncle from doing dumb shit, or letting his temper get out of hand. If two guys like Uncle Silas tried to hook up, I'm thinking it would be a disaster. There has to be give and take. Different areas and types of strength. Otherwise, all you'd do was butt heads constantly. True of any relationship, really."

"I guess you're right." Plus, the more he thought about it, the more he realized his aunts were every bit as intimidating as their husbands, just in other ways.

"And if you're worried that you're the freakiest Compton

just because you like other guys, I'm afraid to tell you that your mother and I have you—and the rest of them—beat by a mile."

Bryant shook his head. This was one competition he didn't need to win. He held up his hands, palms out. He hadn't cared to hear about their sexcapades from Jake, the rumor mill, and definitely not directly from his own father. "You know what. I'm good. That's all I needed to hear."

He straightened up and edged toward the door of his father's office. Sam wasn't about to let that be the end of it, though. "I'm honestly proud of you, son. For more than your grades. Don't forget that, okay?"

"We'll see how this project goes." Bryant struggled to take a deep breath then, the weight of this impending trial growing.

Sam waved him off. "You're in charge and you know what you're doing. All the other ranches are going to be jealous as fuck when we tell them what we're up to. You're going to have a waitlist of future clients once they see the improvements you make. Just wait."

That would be incredible. Could it be that he'd have meaningful work, and a partner to share his life with here, in the place he'd never stopped thinking of as home?

It was too much to hope for.

"Thanks, Dad."

"Anytime. Now go get your laptop and email me a spreadsheet of everything you need and how much it costs. Get your ass to work."

"Yes, sir."

10

———

Today was the day. The day all of Bryant's brainstorming finally became something tangible. Something valuable. It had taken a week for his dad to establish a line of credit for the supplies and for his cousin Austin to be able to haul them back to the ranch after collecting them from various distribution centers across the region. Bryant suspected he might have taken a detour in an attempt to catch Hayden singing at a roadside bar along the way.

Considering Bryant had spent all his nights with Vaughn since the day of Jake's funeral, he couldn't blame Austin for taking whatever chance he got to see the woman he'd fallen for, even if they weren't technically a couple at the moment. Until right then, Bryant hadn't realized how devastating a split could be.

The thought of giving up Vaughn and the time they spent together already made him feel sick. What would he do when the guy decided he'd had enough?

"You need a hand unloading that rig?" Speaking of the hellishly handsome tattoo artist... Vaughn strode over to stand next to Bryant, too close for anyone to mistake his possessiveness. Funny, since Bryant had left Vaughn crashed out in bed when he'd slipped from the apartment over Cowboy Ink not even an hour ago. "Mine are free until the shop opens this evening."

Bryant stared at him and shook his head. It wasn't like he was going to send him away now, but he didn't want to be a burden. He'd already imposed enough, practically moving in with the man and jumping him every moment they were alone.

Vaughn shrugged, as if it was no big deal that he'd caught up and joined Bryant for the initial phase of his experiment.

"Don't you have to sleep sometime?" He knew full well Vaughn hadn't gotten much rest the night before, or the night before that, or the night before that. And he'd sort of been hoping they might have a repeat performance every night for however long he was here and working on this project. Maybe forever, if he was insanely lucky. He didn't want to ask too much of his...

Well, whatever Vaughn was to him—boyfriend, lover, partner, friend?

"Eh. There will be plenty of time for that when I'm old and boring. I'd rather spend the day watching you work in those jeans." Vaughn rubbed his hands together. "That's plenty of relaxation for me."

"Then I must not be doing it right. Otherwise, you'd be riled up instead." Bryant hoped he could drive Vaughn even half as crazy as he felt every time they were together.

"I'm a master of self control." Vaughn nudged him with his elbow. "Come on, Bryant. I know what you're working on is important and I honestly want to help. I'm useful for more than fucking your brains out. Let me be more to you than a stiff cock."

Bryant's heart flip-flopped in his chest. And, honestly, he couldn't afford to turn away assistance.

"Okay. I admit I'm kind of freaking out looking at all this

shit and wondering how the hell I'm going to get it installed in time to meet my thesis deadline." He rubbed his stomach. It churned at the thought of falling down so close to the finish line. "Austin is going to help, too, when he's not out on the road. He made me promise to let him operate the backhoe."

"Damn, I was hoping to do that." Vaughn grinned.

"He'll probably let you have a turn if you give him a discount on that new tattoo he's after." Bryant chuckled.

"Genius, Dr. Compton. Pure genius." Vaughn leaned down as if he would kiss Bryant, right there in broad daylight.

Bryant dodged. The frown Vaughn leveled at him had him saying, "Sorry. I need to focus."

"You sure you're not embarrassed of me?" Vaughn asked, his shoulders bunching up.

"Not in the least." Bryant put his hand on Vaughn's forearm. "I would really appreciate your help. And...your company. I'll try not to get so stressed out that I screw stuff up between us. Please, stay."

"You got it. Anytime." Vaughn smiled. "And if you need me to help you blow off some steam, there are plenty of places to sneak away for a quickie around here."

"I'm going to pretend I didn't hear that," Austin grumbled as he carried the first load of PVC pipes to the area Bryant had designated for them in his hyper-organized and color-coded plans. "If I'm not getting any, no one should be getting any."

Bryant turned away so his cousin couldn't see his cheeks heat. Hopefully Vaughn understood he wasn't used to being the object of flirtatious teasing since he'd been living the monk life for years. When he glanced over his shoulder, he caught a worried look on the guy's face. He'd have to clarify later so Vaughn didn't assume the worst about himself.

Bryant's hang-ups were all his own.

He took his time spreading out his schematics and hammering the project plan to the side of the hay storage facility they were using as his project headquarters. There was plenty of room for them under the massive shelter. At this time of year, their stores were running low. It would only continue to get worse if the summer was as dry as the spring had been. At least until they had Bryant's systems fully functional.

He clenched his jaw as he looked at the 1,247 discrete tasks necessary to complete before he could declare the project finished. Only after reminding himself exactly how much had to be done in so little time did he turn back around.

Austin, Vaughn, and about a half dozen other ranch hands his dad could spare—or at least had claimed he could—were making short work of sorting the supplies and putting them in the designated bins Bryant had set up to keep everything in order.

He undid the buttons at his wrist, then rolled his checked shirt to his elbows.

"Hell yeah. Get those hands dirty," Vaughn murmured as he passed awfully close on his next trip to the trailer. Of course, when he did, he got a look at the plans. All jokes died then.

Vaughn studied them carefully, then read through the summary of each of the major phases—landscaping, retention, soil enhancement, sensor installation, intelligent irrigation, drone monitoring, and catchment. Then he scanned the drawings again. It shouldn't have been a surprise that those made the most sense to him. He turned to Bryant with a new appreciation that turned him on more than anything they'd done in bed.

"It's been a while since I worked on the ranch, but...this isn't like anything I've ever seen before. The feedback from the land itself, data analysis that directs water usage, and this other high-tech shit." Vaughn plucked one of the custom-designed fittings from the bin and compared it to the schematics. "If this really works like you have it shown over here, this could be revolutionary for agriculture."

"I sure hope so." He nodded.

"You're going to make a fortune selling these." Vaughn placed it gently back in the pile even though they weren't that delicate. The programming on the chips that controlled the flow of water, the compounds that retained additional moisture, the proprietary environmental analysis equations, and the sensors—which detected the moisture in the soil and directed water outlays plant by plant—*that* was where the fancy stuff was. "Installing them on other ranches, too."

"Oh. I, uh, hadn't really looked that far ahead." Bryant scratched his head. "I've been focusing on what I could do to make things more stable here."

But now that he thought about it, that wasn't how he'd been raised. Though it might be better for his family if they hoarded the technology he designed in order to give Compass Ranch a competitive advantage, that's not what Jake would have encouraged him to do. The rest of his family either. Maybe he could make more than just their ranch a better place.

Vaughn was right. There was more work to be done. And some profit to be made, most likely. Hell, because of his calculations, Bryant could show any potential customers that they would recoup their money tenfold in the first three years of using his water management systems.

Win-win, he supposed.

With even bigger goals motivating him, they got busy and didn't stop until the sun disappeared and they ran out of stuff they could do under the lights Austin and Vaughn had rigged up on the side of the hay storage area.

Bryant leaned against the wall and crossed two more items off the project plan.

Finally, some real progress.

"Damn, this smart shit is hard work." It was also freakishly hot for early summer. Vaughn wiped sweat from his brow. When he stretched his back, it popped loud enough to make

Bryant wince. His fingers itched to rub it, to ease the knots he'd been responsible for putting there. But he balled them into a fist instead.

What they did in the privacy of Vaughn's apartment was one thing. Out here, on the ranch... Well, he still wasn't sure he was ready to be so bold. Not because he was ashamed of Vaughn, but because there were too many bad memories of what happened when he mixed work with pleasure at this place.

Vaughn looked away. "If you're done with me, I'd better get back to the shop. I delayed my appointments about as long as I dare. The guys are probably over at the bar getting hammered. If I don't get back into town soon, it's going to be a disaster...if it's not already."

"Shit. I didn't realize you did that." Bryant paused, unsure if he should shake Vaughn's hand or let his lover leave at that when what he really wanted to do was hug Vaughn for putting his own responsibilities aside to be there for him. Again.

When he didn't open his arms, Vaughn sighed. "See you tomorrow then. Same time?"

Even after that, he'd still be willing to help. Still be there to support Bryant, just like he'd promised? Damn. Bryant didn't deserve that unwavering allegiance. He'd still take it. "Yeah, but if you're tired..."

"I'll be here." Vaughn tipped his hat at Bryant and Austin, then pivoted on his boot heel.

He'd only gotten a few steps away when Austin glared at Bryant.

"What?" Bryant asked his cousin in a hiss.

"Go talk to him. Don't let him leave alone." Austin nudged Bryant in Vaughn's direction. "No guy volunteers for this bullshit unless he's related or has a thing for the person organizing the project."

If Austin only knew.

Hell, Bryant should talk to his cousins. Things had happened so fast, and they'd had their own issues, so he hadn't had a chance yet. And now wasn't the time or the place for midnight confessions. Soon, though. He would come clean and ask for help because right now it felt like he was screwing up.

So fix it, you idiot, he mentally scolded himself.

"Hey, Vaughn. Hold on a second." He charged after the other man, barely catching up with him before he climbed into his badass truck. It was jet black like Vaughn's hair and his torn jeans and his boots. "How terrible would it be if you canceled those appointments tonight?"

He shrugged. "Like I said, the guys probably have had too many for me to be comfortable inking them anyway. Won't be a huge deal if I push them to tomorrow. That's usually my day off, so I can fit everyone in."

"Do it." Bryant couldn't believe *he* was being the bad influence. "The least I can do is make you dinner for helping out. I'll grab a few steaks from the ranch fridge and enough stuff from Vicki's garden for a salad. What do you say?"

Bryant wondered what Vaughn would say if he knew how badly he wanted to offer himself up as dessert after he'd satisfied the rest of their appetites.

Vaughn looked down at himself and frowned. "I can't eat like this. I'm filthy."

"Sterling and Viho's cottage has a shower. You can use it while I'm cooking." They both paused at that, as if they were imagining the same scene. Vaughn naked and dripping wet as he soaped himself up in the closest thing Bryant had to personal space. If his sister saw Vaughn's truck parked next to Bryant's, she'd keep her distance.

Hell, she'd probably go as far as shooing any other would-be visitors away. Turned out Vaughn and Sterling had become pretty good friends since their shops had opened in such close proximity. If two of the people he liked most on the planet also liked each other, that had to be a good sign, right?

"Let *me* take care of *you* tonight," he said softly.

Vaughn considered for half a second before nodding. "Deal. Take me home, Bryant."

11

———

Vaughn had worked until after midnight the night before, woke his ass up before dawn to make it over to Bryant's place, and then hauled heavy shit around and dug trenches—exactly the sort of back-breaking labor he'd escaped by hustling for so long to build his own business—just to spend as much time as possible with his geeky cowboy obsession. And still, his dick wasn't too tired to persuade him that blowing off clients for a fuck and a famous Compass Ranch steak dinner would be a nice way to round out the long, hard day.

Long and hard, indeed.

He stared at Bryant as the guy stripped his sweat-stained shirt over his head and flicked open the button on his jeans, preparing to wash away the proof of their efforts so that he could slave over a home-cooked meal for Vaughn. Right there, on Compass Ranch, where his truck in the driveway overnight would ensure every damn person knew exactly what they were doing inside. Gossip moved at lightning speed in a place like this. They both knew it, which meant Bryant was deliberately broadcasting their involvement to his family and the rest of their community.

He wasn't ashamed of being associated with Snake's bastard kid.

It didn't take more than that simple fact to disengage Vaughn's brain and fire up every one of his animal instincts. He staggered forward and yanked Bryant's pants to his ankles, then held out his hand so the guy could step from them without losing his balance. Look at him, being all chivalrous and shit.

Bryant brought out things in him no other man ever had. Probably because of his artless attraction to Vaughn, and the way he surrendered to his urges when they were together, something he'd never done in the past.

In this relationship, whatever it was, they were both on unfamiliar ground. It turned Vaughn on to know he was the only person Bryant had shared this intimacy with. It made him feel valued, and special, and honored. All things he'd rarely experienced.

It also made him horny as fuck. He wasn't sure how his dick wasn't chafed by now, but he was glad it wasn't. Because he needed more. Maybe he would never get enough.

He led Bryant into the bathroom, and then the shower.

"What do you think you're doing?" Bryant asked as Vaughn flicked on the water, making warm droplets rain over them both, soaking the clothes he hadn't even bothered to take off yet.

When Bryant covered his hand and snapped the faucet off, Vaughn blinked several times. Was he really getting shut down? Had he read the situation wrong? "You seriously don't want me to fuck you right now? I'm dying to be buried inside you again. Watching how confident you were directing everyone like a well-oiled machine, realizing just how fucking brilliant you really are, and knowing that you still gave me a second chance at this all day has me about to burst. But if you're not into it...or me..."

"What? Hell no. That's not the problem." Bryant reared back, smacking his head on the tile in the process.

Wincing, Vaughn rubbed the fine golden hairs there in apology. "Then what *is* the problem exactly?"

"Wasting water is a boner killer, and I have a feeling we're going to take a while if we...well, you know." Bryant dropped his stare, struggling to adequately describe the feral passion they'd indulged in recently. Vaughn didn't blame him. He'd had way more experience in the bedroom, though none of it half as hot as what he'd shared with Bryant, and yet he couldn't quite explain it either.

How could someone as generous and greedy in bed still be so reserved and endearing the rest of the time?

Vaughn wasn't sure, but he loved that about his new playmate. He grinned and kissed Bryant on the cheek. "You're really fucking cute, you know that?"

Bryant shrugged one shoulder, a hint of his old shyness returning. Vaughn wouldn't stand for that. Oh no. He put his hands on Bryant's shoulders and urged the other man to lean in so that he could seal their mouths together. Right before he did, he rasped, "I'm happy to fuck you dirty, for the sake of the planet and all."

A groan slipped from Bryant's lips just before he nodded vigorously. "Yeah, do that."

"Better yet..." Vaughn growled when he needed to pause to catch his breath. Never before had a man been able to push him so hard with a simple kiss. "Why don't you take your shower while I watch? Go ahead."

Bryant blinked a few times. Vaughn was about to retract his suggestion, afraid of pushing him into things he wasn't ready for or didn't want. But then he realized he might be being overcautious. Part of what had made Bryant defenseless to that monster years ago was his innate tendency to let his sexual partner take control.

It was time to see if that was what he still really wanted. Vaughn said, "Hey, this is me. You can say no at any time and it will never impact what I think of you or how much I want you, okay?"

Bryant nodded.

"So if you don't like something, all you have to do is tell me."

Bryant nodded again.

"And if you don't speak up, I'm going to assume you like what I'm doing. Even when I'm pushy."

"I do." Bryant bit his lip, his cock growing harder with each moment they stood there staring at each other.

"So get in that shower and put on a show for me." Vaughn winked. "A fast one, so we don't waste any of your precious water."

Bryant smiled slow and wide. "I can do that."

While he fiddled with the knobs, adjusting the spray, Vaughn made quick work of his clothes. He hopped from foot to foot as he tugged off his boots and socks, then peeled his jeans off before dropping them and his shirt in a pile on the floor. By the time Bryant had gathered his shampoo and started lathering his hair, causing soapy bubbles to stream down his chest and arms, Vaughn was standing with his feet planted in the bathmat, his cock in hand.

He stroked himself to the sight of Bryant Compton, gloriously naked and looking for all the world like a supermodel. If they featured him in a magazine ad for that shampoo, they'd sell a million extra bottles a minute. Vaughn was glad he wasn't, though, that he could hoard Bryant's sexiness, all for himself.

He'd never felt this sort of greedy lust before.

Another first for him.

Good thing Bryant was hurrying as he ran his hands over every inch of his hard body, because otherwise Vaughn would shoot all over the glass doors instead of deep inside the man who inspired his desire. All too soon, Bryant finished and conscientiously shut off the shower even for the minute it took them to switch places.

"Your turn," Vaughn rasped as he paused to steal a single kiss. "I want you to stand there where I can see you, and show me how much you like looking at me."

Bryant nodded, biting his lower lip. When he curled his hand around his hard-on, he groaned and shivered. Nothing could have motivated Vaughn to hurry more than that. Fuck the planet—he wanted to be in bed with Bryant. ASA-fucking-P.

About the time Bryant cupped his balls in addition to jacking off, Vaughn had finished getting clean. Just in time to get nasty again.

He practically leapt from the shower, grabbed Bryant's wrist, and towed him to the bedroom without bothering to dry off. When they reached the bed, he put his hand on Bryant's shoulder to prevent him from climbing on the mattress.

Instead, he bent Bryant over the edge, then swept his foot between the other man's legs until Bryant got the idea and spread himself wide. He braced his hands on the covers, as if preparing for Vaughn to slide inside him without any preparation. Crazy. He'd never do that to Bryant.

Hell no—he planned to show him another new trick.

Vaughn dropped to his knees behind Bryant and grabbed him around his hips. He held the guy still when he leaned in and began to kiss his lower back and ass, wandering lower to suck on his balls.

Good thing, because Bryant reared up then collapsed, groaning while Vaughn teased him mercilessly. He arranged Bryant's cock so that it was pointed down, just off the edge of the bed. That way he could stroke it and fondle Bryant's balls as he used his other hand to spread Bryant's cheeks.

Vaughn bit Bryant's tight ass, not too hard, then reached out and licked upward from his balls through his crack. When Bryant froze, he paused. "Do you like this?"

"Yes. Fuck yes." Bryant's cock jerked in Vaughn's hand as if trying to prove just how much it turned him on. "Do it again. Please."

Vaughn chuckled against Bryant's hot flesh, then gave him what he asked for. Except he didn't stop there. He used his tongue to probe Bryant's hole, rimming him until he was wet and slippery with saliva. All the while, he fisted Bryant's cock, tugging on it in time to the motion of his mouth. His palm grew slick thanks to the precome leaking from Bryant's tip.

And just when he thought he'd die if he couldn't find some relief of his own, Bryant shouted. "Vaughn! Fuck me. Please. I need it. I need you."

Vaughn practically snarled as he thought about the condom buried in his jeans, somewhere in the pile of clothes in the bathroom. "Hang on. I need to get protection."

"Don't. Not tonight. I don't want anything between us." Bryant moaned. "Fuck me bare."

They hadn't discussed it since their first time, and Vaughn hadn't been about to push it. Bryant knew where he stood, and Vaughn had left it up to the other man to tell him what he wanted. Neither was he going to argue. If that was what Bryant asked for, that was what he was about to get. "Okay."

As soon as Vaughn had one last thing. He couldn't explain the urge he got then, but he only knew things were getting stirred up inside him. Lust, affection, and something else... Inspiration.

"Do you have a pen?" Vaughn asked.

"What?" Bryant shook his head as if to help the question penetrate his passion-hazed mind.

"A pen. Quick." Vaughn closed his eyes to maintain the vision that had flashed through his mind when he saw Bryant laid out on the bed before him.

With one arm, Bryant reached over to the nightstand and slapped his hand around blindly until he clutched a pen in his fingers. He tossed it over his shoulder in Vaughn's direction.

Vaughn didn't hesitate. He ripped the cap off with his teeth, then spat it onto the floor. He aligned his cock with Bryant's ass using his left hand, then pressed deep in a single firm but fluid stroke. Bryant gasped. Still, he rocked back, asking for more despite the rudimentary lube they were using.

Once he was sure Bryant wasn't hurting, but loving the cock in his ass instead, Vaughn leaned forward. He braced his left forearm on Bryant's back then let his right hand, which gripped the pen, fly. It was mindless.

All he concentrated on was rocking into Bryant, over and over, the steady medium pace like keeping time to a song by tapping his toe. As he fucked, his hand took on a life of its own, roaming over Bryant's skin. It traced, outlined, and marked.

Vaughn couldn't say why it was so deeply satisfying to make Bryant look like the living embodiment of the art he'd starred in recently, but it was.

Vaughn grunted and fucked deeper into Bryant's ass. It turned him on to watch the ink spreading over his lover, snaking around his upper arm, forming the undeniable pattern he'd envisioned highlighting Bryant's form. The artwork fit him organically, as well as his own skin, enhancing his natural beauty.

"Turn over," Vaughn demanded with a smack on Bryant's ass. He withdrew his cock only long enough to help his lover change positions.

They groaned in unison when he sank back inside Bryant, filling him completely.

When he normally would have taken the opportunity to

make out with the other guy, instead his hand kept going, this time decorating Bryant's chest.

"What are you drawing?" Bryant shook his head and tried to peer down at Vaughn's handiwork.

"Don't worry about that." Vaughn gasped, then rode Bryant harder, art pouring out of him faster as his rapture mounted. "Just lay back and…"

His hips ground forward, drawing Bryant's attention to what mattered at the moment.

Then they gave up conversation in favor of action. Lots and lots of action.

Vaughn lost himself in the way Bryant made him feel. And he didn't only mean his dick. Being with Bryant impacted him profoundly, opened parts of himself he'd kept locked away for too long. He only hoped he was doing the right thing by making himself as exposed as Bryant had when he finally took what he needed.

Sometime later, Vaughn realized he'd finished. He threw the pen aside and stared into Bryant's wide, glazed eyes. He cupped Bryant's cheeks between his palms, then kissed him long and deep. Bryant's cock jumped, where it was sandwiched between them.

"You're close?" Vaughn asked, though he already knew the answer to his question.

"So close. Feels so good, but I don't want it to be over."

Vaughn rested his forehead on Bryant's, then concentrated on nudging the other man's prostate on each return pass of his cock. "Have to finish so we can start again some other time."

And wasn't that the truth. He hadn't meant to be philosophical, but he thought of the day Bryant had left Compton Pass, and how amazing it was now that he was home again.

He vowed to himself right then and there, that even if something came between them, he'd never give up on trying to make it right again. Because this was life. This was everything.

Vaughn ignored the burn in his thighs and picked up his pace. He made sure to stroke Bryant's cock with his abs as he plunged into him. He squeezed Bryant's ankles, then lifted his legs so that they could come even closer together.

It only took a few strokes in that position to make Bryant shatter.

He stared up into Vaughn's eyes as he let go. And flew.

Bryant groaned in time to the pulses of his cock, which pumped come onto Vaughn's abdomen. The first blast of hot fluid set him off too, and he emptied himself into Bryant so hard he forgot to breathe. When his vision became tinged with blackness, he gasped, drawing air into his lungs until he could shout his release to the exposed rafters.

He stood there, half crumpled over Bryant as the other man caressed his shoulders and helped him come down from the most intense high of his life. When his cock slipped from Bryant's body, along with a trickle of fluid, Bryant sighed.

That soft, wistful sound brought Vaughn back to reality. One where he was crushing Bryant after fucking them both senseless. He rained kisses over Bryant's face before pushing to his feet, where he swayed for a moment, trying to regain some semblance of balance.

Which is when he saw what he had done, fully, for the first time.

"Holy shit," he murmured as he raked his gaze over Bryant's relaxed body.

When his boyfriend—when had he started thinking of Bryant like that?—tried to look down at himself, Vaughn helped him rise from the bed. He walked Bryant over to the old-fashioned oval standing mirror in the corner and stood behind him.

He wrapped one arm around Bryant's middle and the other

at his collarbones, clutching him tight to his chest while dropping light kisses on his shoulder and the crook of his neck. In between his forearms, Bryant's entire torso was decorated in ink. Vaughn had no idea how he'd drawn so much in such a short amount of time, unless they'd fucked a lot longer than he thought while he was in his sex-trance.

"I can't believe you just did this. While we were..."

"Fucking?" Vaughn finished for him, although he'd nearly said *making love* instead. "Because you do things to me that no one else ever has. You pull things out of me that I've only wished existed before. You're turning me into a better me, and I hope I can do the same for you."

Bryant nodded, more solemnly than Vaughn had hoped. "You are."

They stood there together for a while, looking at one example of how their lives might come together. How they might mesh into the perfect intelligent badass duo if they harnessed both of their skills and cancelled out each other's weaknesses.

"Will you take a picture of me? Like this?" Bryant's gaze never left his reflection. "I love the way you see me. The guy I could become if I let you mold me into him."

Somehow Vaughn didn't think they were talking about tattoos anymore.

He left Bryant only long enough to grab his phone off the bedside table, then took his time framing Bryant's gorgeous body and his even more handsome face in the shots. Vaughn knew he'd treasure them forever, no matter what happened after tonight.

"I don't know how I'll ever be able to repay you, for helping me find myself and for all your support here...and on my project." Bryant swallowed hard.

Vaughn felt dangerously close to professing his feelings, and maybe scaring Bryant off. They'd only found each other again a week ago. Too soon for the things he was suspecting. Too many things had changed. They'd lost Jake. Bryant had uprooted his entire life. And they'd each begun to open themselves to the possibility of something…greater, whether physical or emotional.

So he sidestepped.

"You can start with that steak dinner you promised me." Vaughn smacked Bryant on the ass, then aimed him toward the kitchen.

"Now that I can do." Bryant smiled and plucked an apron from a peg on the hook near the stove. The fact that his bare cheeks, red handprint and all, peeked out the back didn't bother either of them in the least. Dinner and a show? Yes, please.

Vaughn ate twice that night. Once, a delicious meal. Then after, he devoured the chef.

12

———

After more than a month of slaving away on the ranch improvements and fucking Vaughn every chance he got, Bryant was utterly exhausted. At precisely four in the morning, he grumbled to Vaughn's home automation system, "Alarm off."

"Snooze for how long?" it responded.

"No snooze. Alarm off." Vaughn answered for him.

Bryant groaned. "I wish I could stay here all day and sleep, but I can't. We're almost finished."

"It'll wait one damn day." Vaughn wrapped his arms around Bryant as if he didn't plan to let him go. "Doug told you last night—there isn't a chance it'll rain for the next week, until that low pressure system works its way over us. Today is going to be the hottest and most miserable yet. You're going to sweat your balls off and I think you're already dehydrated, especially after that marathon last night."

Bryant snorted. They *had* worked up quite a sweat. He didn't want to admit it, but he'd almost been too tired to fool around. Too beat up. They'd been busting their asses nonstop for weeks and he wasn't used to ranch life anymore. It was taking its toll. How Vaughn was keeping up with that and his shop, Bryant had no idea. Though sometimes he'd join Vaughn downstairs, answer phones, clean the place up, and take appointments, most nights he came upstairs and took a nap before rejoining his boyfriend. If Bryant went out to the ranch today, Vaughn would follow.

Maybe if he took the day off, his boyfriend—because there was no doubt now that that's what they were, even if neither of them had said the word out loud—would do the same.

He'd obviously been silent too long.

Vaughn grew serious again. "You can't keep this up. One day, Bryant. Rest. Then you'll be able to bang out the rest of the finishing touches on the system faster, with less chance of making a mistake. How much could that cost you?"

Everything. It was true. All of it.

They'd talked to his cousin at length yesterday, getting the scoop on his current documentary about storm chasing as well as professional input from the very pretty weather expert Doug was following around. Very diligently, in Bryant's opinion. Not that he could blame him, considering how he'd dogged Vaughn's steps every waking moment lately and how that still wasn't enough, despite their near inseparability. Doug had predicted at least one—if not more—additional week of this hellacious dry spell and record-breaking heat wave.

Bryant tried to calm his racing heart. Unlike the wildfires it was causing farther west, which his cousin James had to deal with, the drought wasn't critical here...yet. It was only delaying his research. In the grand scheme of things, everyone was probably right. He needed to relax. Regroup. Then finish his project strong.

"Okay, fine. I will take one day off. *One.*" They really only had a little bit more to go. Hook up a few pipes, seal the joints, turn on the monitoring system, and that was it. The rest was up to nature and ironing out any wrinkles in the automation software.

Waiting to find out if it worked as anticipated was likely to kill him if he didn't distract himself. Fortunately, Vaughn was more than willing to help in that department.

"Smart move." Vaughn smiled widely as he pulled Bryant over him like a blanket.

Bryant settled himself in the place he'd come to love most, lying on his boyfriend's chest. "I thought we were going to rest."

"We will. After we've knocked ourselves out with a few solid orgasms," Vaughn promised.

Bryant hummed. "Good plan. I want to see if morning sex is as amazing as everyone says it is."

After a few lazy kisses, Vaughn said. "I'd like to find that out myself."

"What do you mean?" Bryant narrowed his eyes. Surely Vaughn had done it a million times. He'd seen the looks they'd gotten from guys in the shop or even around town. There were plenty of men jealous as hell of Bryant for monopolizing Vaughn's sex life lately.

"You're the only person I've ever invited to stay over. And the only person I've ever hooked up with more than once," Vaughn admitted, rubbing his thumb over Bryant's lower lip.

Waaaaaaaaaay more than once. Hell, more than once a day.

"Really?" Bryant reared back, taking in Vaughn from an arm's length. "Why me?"

Vaughn shrugged then reached for him, pulling him back. Instead of answering, Vaughn kissed the shit out of Bryant, making him forget why it mattered. All he cared about was their chemistry and making the bond between them burn bright.

Deciding he wanted to show Vaughn he understood what a big deal it was, he shifted and trailed his lips down Vaughn's neck, then his chest and his abs. He didn't think he'd ever admit it to his cousins, but Bryant enjoyed sucking Vaughn's cock nearly as much as he did receiving a blowjob. Of course, sixty-nine was his absolute favorite. But not this morning.

This morning he wanted Vaughn to bask in Bryant's devotion and know just how much he was appreciated. He had spent a good amount of time rubbing Vaughn's cock idly as he licked at the solid six-pack beneath him, when something rumbled.

At first Bryant thought it might be his stomach, or Vaughn's, but then the deep bass reverberated through the walls.

"Did you hear that?" Bryant asked.

"All I hear is my cock wishing you'd hurry the fuck up." Vaughn speared his hands into Bryant's hair, using the grip to guide his mouth closer to the tip of his fat cock.

Bryant grinned. "Not that. I thought I heard thunder in the distance."

"Just a delivery truck going by. They restock the grocery store across the street at the ass crack of dawn every Tuesday. Ignore it." Vaughn waved him away. "Be here fully. Stay with me, Bryant."

It was a sign of Bryant's desperation that even while fooling around with the sexiest boyfriend a guy could ask for, he was—somewhere in the back of his mind—still dwelling on his project. "Sorry."

"Don't be. Just get over here and let me help you forget about all that." Vaughn tugged Bryant closer, his erection brushing the seam of Bryant's lips.

Bryant parted them and licked the warm, satiny skin in front of him.

After groaning, Vaughn said, "I wish you were as obsessed with me as you are with that damn thesis."

"I am. Believe me, I am. I swear. Here, let me show you." He leaned in and took Vaughn's cock in his mouth. Soon enough, he forgot all about the clock ticking on his assignment. There'd be plenty of time later to finish it up.

Time when he didn't have utter control over his boyfriend's pleasure. Maybe that was why he loved going down on the guy so much. He knew that in these moments, he was in charge. Sure, Vaughn might be fucking up into his mouth, or holding his face where he liked it, but Bryant was the one driving him wild. He experimented with different grips, various motions of his tongue, and the addition of his fingers playing with Vaughn's balls until he found the perfect recipe. He could draw things out or make Vaughn come quickly, whatever he liked.

Right then, he chose to extend the moment so that he could look up at the hard plane of muscles flexing and bulging while Vaughn's head was thrown back. The hitch in his breathing and the rock-hard quads that cradled Bryant between them were all thrilling.

He got off on bringing his partner so damn much pleasure.

His own cock throbbed beneath him, begging for the relief he knew Vaughn would be generous in returning once he'd recovered from what Bryant hoped was the most amazing blowjob of his life.

Without thinking, he slid his hand between Vaughn's legs and below his tight sac. He ran his finger between Vaughn's ass cheeks and was surprised when the other guy didn't tense. Instead, he spread his legs farther and gave Bryant better access, which he used to both their satisfaction.

He'd barely begun to prod Vaughn's ass, rubbing circles around it in between forays into forbidden territory, when his partner froze. Without the usual warning he gave, he drew Bryant's mouth down his entire length, then shot hard and fast, glazing Bryant's tongue with his come.

The intensity of his reaction impressed Bryant. It also turned him on. To know he could do that to Vaughn. He flexed his hips, rubbing his cock on the sheets a few times, surprised when his own orgasm overtook him without anyone even touching his dick.

Bryant unloaded on the bed while Vaughn murmured reassurance that it was okay to lose control. They fed off each other, and that would never be a bad thing. When the spasms subsided, Bryant collapsed with his head on Vaughn's torso and the other man's cock still in his mouth.

He suckled it gently until it softened, loving the way Vaughn stroked his hair and rubbed his back the entire time.

Eventually Bryant stretched, prepared to climb up so he could snuggle into Vaughn's open arms and make good on his promise to sleep the day away.

Until he heard something that didn't make any sense.

Bryant paused, but this time the sound of dripping water only got louder. "Is the faucet leaking or something?"

Vaughn's eyes widened, triggering Bryant's alarm. He froze momentarily before bolting from bed and dashing to the windows to rip aside the blackout curtains. Outside, rivulets poured across the glass, the sky gray and unfriendly behind it.

"It's raining!" The moment Bryant had been waiting for had come, at exactly the wrong time. "Fuck! We're not ready! The system isn't complete, the circuit isn't closed. We're not capturing any of it."

He grabbed his jeans from the floor, then started hopping into them as he made his way to the door. He didn't even have his boots all the way on before he grabbed his keys out of the little bowl he'd gotten used—*too* used—to storing them in on Vaughn's counter, then stumbled down the staircase.

What had he done?

Had he missed his chance because he'd been too busy fooling around to finish the job?

"Bryant, wait!" Vaughn yelled into the storm from the doorway.

"I already waited too long. Fuck, thanks to you...I'm even

more fucked than when you're buried in my ass." He snarled as his brain flipped into the old pattern it had been stuck in for so long. Once again his dick had led him straight down a path of horrific decision-making.

When the hell would he learn?

Then Vaughn was there beside him, grabbing his shoulders. "I'm sorry. Let me help you fix this. If we go now, maybe we can seal up that last section of pipe before it stops."

"I've got it." Bryant wrested his shoulders free of Vaughn's grasp and began running. For the truck, for Compass Ranch... anything away from the mess he'd made. "You *helped* enough."

Vaughn looked as though he might argue, standing there drenched, his bare chest glistening with the rain they'd needed so badly. But just then the downpour abated, trickling off to a shower, then a drizzle, and lastly a few lingering spatters in a matter of moments.

"Son of a bitch!" Bryant threw his hat at his truck. This couldn't be happening. He watched a gush of water swirling down the storm drains, completely wasted.

"Bryant—" Vaughn tried one last time to convince him this wasn't a complete disaster. It was futile.

"Go take care of yourself, Vaughn. You think I didn't see those negative reviews your system emailed in last night from the out-of-town friends who couldn't get appointments? You're spending too much time with me and neglecting your business." They'd been foolish, both of them, and risked too much. It might be too late for Bryant's project, but he wasn't about to take Vaughn down with him.

If the guy couldn't do the right thing for himself, then Bryant would do it for him.

Because, despite everything, Bryant cared. A hell of a lot. It sucked that that wasn't enough to matter sometimes.

Vaughn nodded slowly. "Come back when you're finished. Okay?"

Rather than lie, Bryant didn't say anything at all. He didn't even look at Vaughn when he hopped into his truck and headed for home.

The silence as he drove back to Compass Ranch alone for the first time in what seemed like forever gave him a lot of room to think. He tried not to recall Vaughn's laughter, or the way he sang along to the radio most mornings, or how they'd had to pull over for a quickie a couple times because even a few hours with their hands off each other seemed like far too long most days. He snarled at the rainbow that appeared in front of him, unable to enjoy it without Vaughn to share it with. It just didn't seem the same. None of it did.

How hadn't he realized how entangled their lives had become? And how dangerous that could be?

Bryant slammed his truck door when he reached the project site, then grabbed his tools. He was about an hour in when his dad popped his head through the access panel into the area where he was connecting the last of the PVC pipes.

"I'm guessing that grimace means you didn't catch the shower?" Sam sighed.

"Sorry, Dad. I should have—"

His dad slapped his hat on his thigh. "That wasn't an accusation, son. You've been busting your ass on this thing for weeks. Sometimes nature doesn't cooperate with a rancher's plans. We'll get the next one."

Bryant nodded. "Can we make it another few weeks without rain?"

"Yeah. After that we'll have to start letting some of the hay go to keep the animals safe." Sam shrugged as if that wasn't another huge financial hit when they'd already outlaid a ton of cash for Bryant's work. "But what about your school stuff?"

He shook his head. "It's due at the end of the week. I'll have to hand in what I have and hope that's good enough."

Acid bubbled in his gut at the thought. They'd already

given him a two-week extension. He couldn't ask for more. Hell, graduation was only ten days from now and he still had to defend his work. In person. His time on the ranch was short. Maybe it was for the best he'd put some space between him and Vaughn now.

"It's good enough for me and your mom, your uncles, and everyone else around here. You remember that. No matter what happens." Sam put his hand on Bryant's shoulder and squeezed. "You're doing your best. That's all I've ever asked of you."

Bryant thought of Vaughn's face as he'd stood there, dripping in the rain while Bryant shouted at him. After all he'd done to help, he hadn't deserved that. It definitely hadn't been one of Bryant's finest moments. But if he wasn't ready to handle those tough times, maybe he shouldn't be screwing around with Vaughn either.

He was a mess. Still broken inside, no matter how much he'd tried to hide it these past several weeks.

Once he'd had time to calm down, he realized that the brief shower wouldn't have been enough to prime the system, even if they'd already finished it. But still, the reminder of his poor judgment and the lengths he'd go to just to get off was a solid kick in the ass.

Bryant finished taking pictures, documenting the last of the installations. He saved them and shot them off in an email to the head of his department. That was it. They either accepted his work and granted him his doctoral degree, or they'd send him packing.

Either way, his college career was over.

He'd lost a big part of how he'd defined himself, and it was making him testy. His thoughts and emotions were scattered and confused as he suddenly found himself adrift.

Which was why it sucked extra bad when he realized he'd missed about a dozen calls and texts from Vaughn, his phone on silent while he'd completed his work. As he should have done early that morning. He wasn't Vaughn's bitch. He was a fucking scientist. One who should be able to think straight, even when his mind was being addled by hormones.

If he couldn't do that, then maybe he needed to take a step back.

They needed to take a break until he could think clearly again.

Bryant stood, dusted off his jeans, then headed over to Sterling's cottage to pack his stuff. He was going back to school to defend his thesis and finish what he'd set out to do. Maybe then he could be confident enough, independent enough, *man* enough to handle being Vaughn's partner.

13

It was an even longer, disturbingly quiet drive from Compass Ranch back to Bryant's university.

Although Vaughn had sent a text offering to ride with him, he'd ignored it. He needed to do this on his own. Finish what he had started. Claim the title he'd dedicated the last half-decade of his life to earning. Make his family proud. Make Jake proud. Damn it, make *himself* proud.

Vaughn couldn't afford to neglect his shop either.

Bryant hadn't been away from school all that long, weeks compared to the years he'd spent on campus, but already he felt like a foreigner in his dusty truck and well-worn cowboy hat. Before he'd last headed home, he'd packed up all his belongings and sublet his apartment to another grad student, so he didn't even have a place to freshen up before heading to the school's science complex. He walked into the hydrology department a cowboy, ducked into the bathroom, and emerged as a doctoral candidate, complete with a tailored suit and tie. His other life tucked neatly in his rolling laptop case.

It was sort of like being Superman in reverse.

He stared down at his dress shoes, missing the comfort of his broken-in boots.

Suddenly he wasn't sure he fit anywhere anymore, in limbo between his academic stomping grounds and the home he'd never be able to fully run away from. He tried to get his head on straight so that he could present his work in the best possible light.

Given the incomplete experiment and his lack of results, he was going to have to fight hard.

He thought of Vaughn and how he'd built Cowboy Ink from the ground up, how tough it must have been for an outsider to establish himself as a legitimate business owner in their tiny country town. Bryant wished he had a little more of that grit right then. He thought of his father, the investment he'd been willing to wager on this, and—of course—he thought of Jake.

Bryant loosened his tie a bit, jammed his hands in his pockets, and mustered some Compass spirit. While he acted like nothing could stop him, he didn't exactly feel the same way when he approached the department chair's office and Dr. Burgess's assistant ushered Bryant into a conference room full of the most brilliant minds in his field.

"Welcome back, Bryant." Dr. Burgess, his favorite professor, stood and shook his hand. "The labs haven't been the same without you there twenty-four-seven."

He supposed he had been a fixture in the study spaces for years now. And all that effort was now riding on the line. "I had to leave the nest sometime. I can't wait to show you all what I've been doing and how my research has translated to the ranch environment."

"We've had a look at the supplemental materials you submitted and would love to hear your full presentation." Dr. Burgess leaned forward, giving Bryant his rapt attention for the next hour and a half. Like always, when Bryant got caught up in his work, everything else faded away.

It was how he'd lived in denial, and isolation, for so long.

When he'd wrapped up his research, he delivered his conclusions. He suppressed a wince when he said, "And so you can see that as soon as it rains, Compass Ranch will be in a greatly improved position. I anticipate that we will consume half as much water as before, recycle a large portion of that, and sustainably store enough reserves to keep the system primed for two years without any additional precipitation."

It was only a couple phrases different from what he knew would have guaranteed victory, but if he could just have had concrete evidence instead of more conjecture, he'd have felt a lot better about his efforts. Fuck anyone who said climate change wasn't real. If anything, this situation only reinforced the rising importance of the technology he'd developed.

He prayed his professors felt the same way.

Dr. Burgess beamed as he said, "I want you to understand how impressed we are with what you've done here, especially in such a short amount of time. It's truly remarkable."

"I had a lot of help. From my family, and...guys on the ranch. I couldn't have done it alone."

"Even still, your thesis project is extremely ambitious and profoundly impactful—or at least it will be when it's complete, if it functions as expected." To hear that from a scientist as respected as Dr. Burgess pumped Bryant up.

He stood straighter. "Thank you, sir."

"In fact, we believe it will be some of the most valuable work to come from one of our alumni. I wouldn't be at all surprised if it earns you several awards and recognition in the field at large. Your record shows that the likelihood of success is almost certain." Dr. Burgess smiled, as the other professors nodded their agreement, while flipping through the images of the new landscaping, the empty retention ponds, and the pipes for the intelligent irrigation systems.

Alumni! Bryant barely withheld his sigh of relief. He had

imagined this moment for so long he could already hear the words about to come out of Dr. Burgess's mouth. *Congratulations, Dr. Compton.*

Except instead, he said, "All of this combined explains why we're extending your project timeline once more to allow it to come to fruition instead of flunking you for handing in an incomplete project."

Dr. Burgess steepled his fingers, then stared down his nose at Bryant over the top of his glasses. His disappointed gaze hit Bryant in the gut along with his verdict.

"An extension? But graduation is less than a week away, and there's still no rain in the forecast." He tipped his head, feeling denser than ever in his life before.

"Commencement is Saturday for students with successfully completed and approved thesis projects." Dr. Burgess turned stony-faced. "You won't be taking part in the hooding ceremony with the rest of this semester's successful candidates, I'm afraid. Finish your project properly over the next several months, or however long it takes, and I'm sure you'll be valedictorian of the next class."

"Next—?" Bryant blinked.

They weren't passing him. He wasn't graduating. Not now, and maybe not ever.

Dr. Compton? Fuck no. He was just Bryant. A loser who hadn't lived up to his potential.

His entire world shattered again, like it had the day in the barn when he'd learned that he wasn't as strong as he thought. Or like it had the day Jake had died, when he learned he didn't have as much time as he thought. Or like it had the day he'd walked away from Vaughn, and learned he wasn't as independent as he thought. Today, he wasn't as smart as he'd thought.

And that was the only thing he'd felt sure about in his life.

He was lost.

Bryant stumbled from the room, ignoring the voices calling out for him to return. He staggered down the hallway of the place that had been his refuge and was now just another hell.

What would he tell his family?

What would he tell Vaughn?

Bryant swallowed back bile when his phone buzzed in his pocket. On autopilot, he took it out and peeked at the screen.

As if he was still as connected to Bryant as he had been when they'd shared a bed, Vaughn reached out again. *How did it go?*

Bryant figured Vaughn would get the picture if he simply didn't answer. Besides, he didn't have the words to express how epically he'd crashed and burned. Come so close, then fucked up right at the finish line.

Where he'd been starting to doubt his decision to walk away from Vaughn and what they'd been building together, now he knew he'd done the right thing.

The fact that he wanted to run back to the guy, even now, cemented his conviction.

14

———

Vaughn had never been this nervous to talk to a guy before. He tapped his fingers on the steering wheel of his truck and gently rubbed the sore area beneath the bandage on his chest, just over his heart. He rumbled over the gravel section of the farm road that led back to where Bryant was holed up. Sterling had unofficially given him a heads-up that Bryant had gotten home safe a few hours ago.

While he was disappointed Bryant hadn't rushed over to share his good news, he didn't let that deter him from going after what he wanted. What he knew, deep down, was the best for them both.

In his mind, Vaughn heard Jake's ancient advice to him, from when he'd first kicked around the idea of opening a tattoo shop. *"You could waste time waiting for the stars to align or you could get out there and start kicking them into place."*

He only hoped that being assertive wouldn't scare Bryant off again. Fuck if he didn't miss the nerd. It made sense since Vaughn had probably spent more time with Bryant than all the other guys he'd slept with in his life. He was officially addicted and not ashamed to admit it.

Even to Bryant's sister, whom he'd poured his heart out to over coffee yesterday, which was why she'd taken pity on him and tipped him off. He owed her a big fat Christmas present, or maybe another tattoo.

With a six-pack of Bryant's favorite beer in hand, he ambled up to the door, took a deep breath, then knocked. When there was no answer, he banged again, this time louder. He would not be ignored. If Bryant wanted him to go, fine. But Bryant should at least be mature enough to tell him to his face and explain why. Surely he couldn't still be upset about missing that tiny rain shower. It wouldn't have been enough to prime the system even if they'd had time to finish the piping that morning, which they hadn't.

No, Bryant was running scared again. Damn if Vaughn would let another six years go by before he pulled Bryant's head out of his ass.

He was about to pound his fist on the door when it jerked open.

Good thing he didn't punch Bryant in the nose by accident. That probably wouldn't help his case. Caught by surprise, it took him a second to realize something was off. Really wrong. At barely after noon, Bryant was...drunk? His eyes were bloodshot and he reeked of alcohol. Sure, they sometimes had a drink or two, but Vaughn had never seen him like this—out of control and miserable.

"Bryant? Are you okay?"

"You brought me more beer? Awesome." He slurred as he lunged for the six-pack in Vaughn's hand, nearly crashing into the door in the process.

"Holy shit." Vaughn steadied him, then half-carried him into the cottage's kitchen. "Are you celebrating by yourself?"

"Celebrating? Fuck no." Bryant plopped into a chair at the table, tipping it precariously before it clunked into place once more.

"Wait..." Vaughn hadn't even considered the possibility that Bryant wouldn't pass with flying colors. "Are you saying—?"

"That they didn't approve my thesis? Yup. I'm not graduating."

Vaughn's insides felt like they'd been flash-frozen. "*Ever*?"

"Who knows?" Bryant shrugged. "Maybe someday. But definitely not next weekend."

"Oh shit." Vaughn reached out to hug Bryant, but the other man flinched instead of leaning into his embrace, so he stopped dead then backed off.

Bryant reached for one of the beers on the table between them and used the edge of Sterling's table to rip the top off before downing half the contents in a single glug. Whoa.

Vaughn was suddenly even more glad he'd come. Bryant shouldn't be alone like this.

"Hey, it's okay. You're going to wait until it rains and then gather the data you need to show them just how fucking lucky this ranch is to have you and your work." Vaughn bent down slowly until they were eye-to-eye, Bryant's mouth within kissing range. "I missed you, you know. I'm happy to distract you. And hey, last time it seemed like we brought the rain when we hooked up. Maybe we can do it again."

Bryant reared back as if Vaughn had hit him instead of hitting on him.

"I don't think that's a good idea. My dick is a terrible decision maker." Bryant looked away, as if even he didn't believe the bullshit he was spouting.

Vaughn tried to chalk it up to his intoxication—dumb shit from the mouth of a drunk man—but he knew it was more than that. Bryant was regressing, falling back into his old habits of blaming himself for shit out of his control. Except this time, Vaughn couldn't help since he was part of the problem.

"Go home, Vaughn. I'm not what you're looking for." He

scrubbed his hands over his face, then stared out the window at the ranch with unfocused eyes.

It made Vaughn ache and pissed him off at the same time.

"You know what…you're right. You're not the man I thought you were." Vaughn shook his head and turned toward the door. He'd let Sterling and Viho know that Bryant was out here, drinking himself into a blackout, and needed someone to watch over him. Someone other than Vaughn.

Which stung like a motherfucker.

Bryant sobered up enough to ask, "What's that supposed to mean?"

"You're a fighter. A person who overcomes. A really fucking sharp guy. Or at least I thought you were all of those things. Yet here you are, wallowing over a temporary setback. Letting it blind you to all the good around you. I'm not going to sit here and join your pity party."

"Good. You weren't invited anyway." Bryant shrugged. The glimmer of regret in his glassy eyes made Vaughn try one last ditch maneuver.

"Sucks that I finally broke down and got my first tattoo and now I'm probably going to have to get it lasered off." He groaned, not exaggerating his remorse at the thought of erasing it. Okay, so he admitted to himself that whether or not Bryant liked the tattoo, and regardless of what he said in anger, he'd never get rid of it, because it—and what it represented—still mattered to him.

Despite having gone off the rails, Bryant—and the brief affair they'd had—had rocked Vaughn's world. It had changed him indelibly. So his skin should reflect the irreversible changes inside him. No matter what happened, he would carry Bryant and memories of what they'd shared with him always.

"You got a tattoo?"

Vaughn cleared his throat. "Technically, I gave myself one, yes. Would you like to see it?"

It was a dare. Even drunk, Bryant had to know it. He narrowed his eyes and paused long enough that Vaughn thought Bryant would kick him out before caving to his innate curiosity. But he didn't. "Sure, what the hell?"

Vaughn yanked the neckline of his black T-shirt down and peeled back the bandage there, exposing the skin above his heart to the man who already owned it.

Bryant didn't make a peep. Didn't move. Didn't do....anything at all.

Was he in shock? Vaughn had to admit he hadn't imagined himself doing something this reckless and permanent...ever, really. Until Bryant.

He'd given himself a tattoo. Which wasn't as easy as he'd anticipated, given the location. But even if it meant a slightly squiggly line here or there, he hadn't wanted anyone else to do it. The most meaningful ink had nothing to do with the prettiest. He should know.

"It's my name," Bryant finally whispered.

Vaughn nodded.

"On you."

He nodded again.

"Forever. I mean, unless you...laser..."

And damn it if Vaughn wasn't starting to get more annoyed. This was in no way how he imagined his big reveal might go. "Is that a problem? No water was harmed in the making of this tattoo, I promise."

"It's just really...real." Bryant rocked onto the back legs of the kitchen chair. "Wow."

Vaughn felt like a fool. He should have known he would never be good enough for Bryant Compton. He figured that Bryant might cool off after he went back to school and realized that everything was fine. Instead of elevating them both, Vaughn had ended up dragging Bryant down to his level. He'd been kidding himself.

Showing Bryant his heart meant nothing, because it was only a reminder of moments that had ruined his life. *Fuck.*

Vaughn had to get out of there. Had to figure out what to do when what he needed most wasn't what was best for the man he loved.

"Goodbye." Vaughn hated that even now he waited for the slightest hesitation on Bryant's part. Maybe he would call Vaughn back. Maybe he would say it was all some terrible joke. Maybe he would decide love mattered more than anything else.

He didn't. Instead Bryant whispered, "Have a nice life."

15

It had been a miserable summer, every day hotter and drier than the last. August had turned downright hellacious and dusty. Like Bryant's sex life. There were tumbleweeds rolling through that shit. And it was his own damn fault.

He didn't remember all of their discussion from the day they'd broken up, but the sight of his name tattooed on Vaughn's chest was burned into his soul. He wasn't sure any more that he'd made the right decision, but too much time had gone by now for him to do anything about it, right?

Bryant flung an arm over his face. He was crashed out on the couch in Sterling's cottage. Stuck. Like he had been all those years before, except now he didn't even have school to distract him.

Without knocking, someone barged through the front door. It could only be one of his family members. "Hey, what if I'm naked in here?"

"You're too boring for that," Doug said as he tromped through the kitchen then plopped down beside him, jarring him.

"Even if you were, it would save a step," Austin said. From behind him, Hayden waved.

"Do I want to know what you're talking about?" Bryant frowned. They were too much right now. Too much when his brain just wanted to sleep the summer away. Maybe longer.

James and Ivy joined the crowd, making the tiny cottage seem like it was going to explode at the seams before James filled him in. "We're taking the girls to check out the new rope swing some of the hands installed in the back pond. It's hot enough that I feel like I'm jumping into a fire again out there. We need a good old-fashioned naked swim break. Come on, you know you want to go. For old times' sake."

Bryant thought about the summer he'd drooled over Vaughn every chance he got, and how—unknown to him—Vaughn had been doing the same. What if Vaughn had gone swimming with them on the day of the now-infamous skinny dip?

Gah! If he didn't stop thinking about Vaughn, he was going to go insane. He might as well let his cousins distract him for a few hours. "Okay, fine. I'm coming."

Bryant got up and shuffled into the bedroom to ditch his shirt and grab a towel. He knew something was up when the loudmouth fuckers he'd grown up with suddenly grew hushed. They whispered frantically among themselves. Oh fuck, what were they up to?

He charged into the living room bare-chested, in time to see them ogling the pictures he'd printed and left on the coffee table. Shit, how had he forgotten they were on display?

Bryant had spent half the evening the night before staring at them, tracing the lines that suited him so well.

"What's this?" Doug asked, holding one up.

"Doesn't matter." He tried to snatch it back, but his cousin dodged.

"I hope James doesn't mind me saying you look fucking hot

like this, Bryant." Ivy glanced between the images and Bryant in the flesh.

Austin held his fist out. "I didn't know you were thinking of joining the ranks. This matches really well with what Vaughn did on me and James. That will be awesome. Kind of like our dads. It's going to take a lot of time, pain, and cash—or blowjobs, if that's your thing. Hope you're prepared."

"It's just a drawing." Bryant shook his head and turned away from them. It hurt to see himself the way Vaughn did. No...*had*.

"You're so full of shit, I can smell it from here." Doug stood up. "Vaughn drew this. He sees something in you that no one else does. Why are you blind to that? You're supposed to be the smart one, but this whole summer you've been acting dumb as dirt."

"This is about more than a tattoo." Hayden linked her hand with Austin's. Bryant was definitely outnumbered. It seemed Vaughn had a fan base among his family, and he didn't mean just his sister, who'd been harping on him for weeks already. "One of the most important things about a partner, is finding someone who believes in you. Someone who knows just how incredible you can be and helps you reach that potential. If it weren't for Austin, I'd never have had the courage to start singing professionally. If Vaughn is that person for you, if he makes you confident, strong, and satisfied, I'm not sure why you're not begging him to come back."

"That's not what Austin did. When you needed freedom, he gave it to you." Bryant stared at the happy couple, remembering what it felt like when he was in their position.

"Did Vaughn ask to be left alone? Or did you?" James wondered.

Bryant didn't answer. He didn't have to. They all knew the truth. Or most of it.

Maybe it was time he told them why he was so fucking scared of making mistakes, even if he was starting to suspect he'd made the worst one of his life recently. "Can we sit down for a second?"

Austin, James, and Doug shared a knowing glance. This was serious shit.

His cousins and the women they loved didn't argue then. They settled in and gave him their full attention.

It was harder to say than he thought, even after all this time. "When I was seventeen, I was raped in the main barn by the big house."

Doug cursed and James just blinked as if he couldn't believe it. That something so awful could happen here, on their beloved ranch.

"Jesus, why didn't you tell us?" Austin asked even as Hayden put her hand on his knee. She paused just long enough to let him nod first, and let her know that was fine.

"I guess I felt like an idiot. Like it was my fault. See, I was trying to hit on Vaughn and he turned me down. Because I wasn't old enough and he's not a scumbag." Bryant shrugged one shoulder. Now that he'd started telling them his worst secret, it seemed like less of a big deal. The power it had held over him disappeared as the words flew from his lips. "But one of the other guys, a new hand, overheard and twisted my disappointment and the rejection I felt. He used it against me, conning me into making out with him...and then didn't take no for an answer when things got out of hand. It would have been a lot worse if Jake hadn't shut things down."

"Oh, fuck," James whispered.

"That's why you didn't date for so long," Austin added. It wasn't a question.

"I didn't intend for it to be that way. I just...focused on school and keeping to the goals I'd set. Made good decisions." He wrung his hands. "At least until I came home and ran into Vaughn again."

"Do our parents know?" Doug wondered aloud at the same

time James asked, "Who was the fuckface that attacked you? Did he ever get what was coming to him?"

"Sorry. Can we talk about that stuff some other time?" Bryant winced. "It's still difficult."

"Of course." Austin nodded. "I'm glad you finally felt like you could tell us."

"I need you to understand why I did what I did. With Vaughn, I mean." He scrubbed his hands over his face. "The very first time I caved to my urges...catastrophe. This time, it might have cost me my degree. When sex is involved, I clearly can't think straight."

"Don't even put those two things in the same category. Hooking up with Vaughn was the *best* thing you've done in forever." Doug lifted the picture up and studied it again. "You two are a great match. A perfect balance. He knows how to deal with you and make you understand what we all know..."

James nodded, taking over for Doug mid-sentence, as they often did with each other. "You're awesome exactly how you are. You don't have to be like every other cowboy on Compass Ranch to deserve happiness. This drawing and these pictures he took of you...they're different, and not only because of the ink. Look at the way you're standing, the way you carry yourself when you're with him. You're a different person. The person you were meant to be. I'm sorry I didn't notice that before."

"I hope you'll let us know when you're struggling with this. I wish we could have been there for you," Austin said as he squeezed Hayden's hand. He'd just recently helped her out of a bad situation with her ex, one that had left her battered. She hadn't broken, and neither would Bryant. Vaughn had helped him see that.

Truth was, Bryant missed being the person he was with Vaughn. He hadn't gotten to wear that skin for very long before things had gone to shit, but for the brief time he had... Well, those had been the best days of his life so far.

Until he'd hit a pothole. And he'd broken down again. Without making any progress. Letting people, including Jake and the rest of his family, down.

"You *were* there for me, guys." He looked around at his cousins, hoping they could see the truth in his eyes. "You've never treated me differently because I'm gay. And I guess that's part of why I didn't say anything. I didn't want it to change things between us. Or for you to see me as weak. I'd already lost enough."

"In that case, I'm going to say what I would say to any of these other assholes if they were fucking something up..." Doug glared at Bryant. "You need to do something to show Vaughn that you want him. And for more than his cock. It's got to be something huge, since you've been jerking off all summer, letting things get out of hand."

"Since when are you the relationship expert?" James smacked Doug on the back of the head. "As far as I can tell, you've been chasing your tail when it comes to your own love life. Maybe you should do as you say, huh?"

Doug grumbled something Bryant couldn't understand under his breath.

He laughed, feeling for the first time in months like things might be okay. Not today, but eventually, if he worked hard enough to make it so.

"As much as I agree with James, I think Doug is on to something." Austin brought him back to reality. "I think you should take some time to consider your options then make a grand gesture. After all, James told me Vaughn got a tattoo of your name. That's pretty serious shit. Especially since I know for a fact he doesn't have any other ink."

"He showed you?" Bryant asked James.

"Uh, yeah. He was trying to talk me out of getting Ivy's name on me in case...you know, things didn't go well when I tried to win her back." He winced. "Sorry."

That news stabbed Bryant in the heart. Did Vaughn regret more than the tattoo? Did he regret his liaison with Bryant all together? There was only one way to find out. He was going to have to man up and ask. Be the person in those pictures.

"Come on." Ivy nudged Bryant. "Let me see this swimming hole everyone's been raving about. You can think about it some and then go to him when you're fully prepared to fight."

Bryant nodded. He was so glad to have their company and to finally have everything out in the open. Maybe someday, with all of their support, he could manage to explain to his parents and the rest of their family how wounded he'd been and why he'd distanced himself. It might alleviate some of his guilt for staying away so long.

It felt right that they were all here, together again. Maybe for good. James had only been home a week or two, but was already fitting in like he'd never left. Austin and Hayden, too. Hell, even Doug was taking a quick break from the storm-tracking crew, due to the fact there were no storms to track.

But that could change. Soon, they hoped.

Until then, he'd enjoy having them around. It felt like the old days, but even better. If Vaughn were there, to finally go skinny dipping with them, it would be perfect. Now Bryant just had to convince Vaughn of that, and he thought he might know just the way to do it, too.

16

Bryant choked up on the neck of the bottle of whiskey in his hand. He hoped Vaughn's favorite liquor would be a peace offering and not a necessity to drown his sorrows in later.

He was about to knock on Vaughn's door when it opened. The guy stepped out far enough to snatch the bottle out of his hands, then set it on the counter barely inside. He crossed his arms as he rejoined Bryant on the landing. "Since when do you drink the hard stuff?"

Damn, Bryant had forgotten about the camera built into Vaughn's home automation software. Had the other guy been watching him as he stood out here, gathering his courage? Was he worried Bryant had spiraled out of control? Bryant wouldn't blame him after their last encounter. "Figured if this doesn't go well I at least owed you a drink for ruining your day off."

"What is *this* exactly?" Vaughn asked.

"Me groveling." Bryant prepared to admit his mistakes, though he dreaded the repercussions. "I know I fucked up majorly when I shut you out. And I...damn, Vaughn, I miss you. I'm so sorry. I should have trusted enough in us to know we'd make it through that shitstorm together. But I freaked out. It's hard not to fall back into bad habits. I blamed myself for getting so caught up in our affair that I might have shortchanged my project, even though I realize now that's not what happened. We did everything we could. Sometimes it's just not enough."

Today might be one of those times. But God, he hoped not.

Vaughn scrunched his eyes closed. Bryant reached out, but let his hand drop. He didn't have the right to touch the other guy or offer his comfort. He'd given up all those perks when he'd shoved Vaughn away. Whether or not he was granted those privileges again was up to Vaughn. Not him.

"Don't take this the wrong way, Bryant." Vaughn kicked at some imaginary rock on the landing. "I'm not sure I can take that chance again. I opened myself up to you, more than with anyone before. And you left me hanging. I won't be able to handle it. You know, if we get back together and you revert to your old self again. The next time something goes wrong in our lives, how will you react? It's been hard this summer—*really fucking hard*—to be so attached to you and then…nothing. I need a partner who will stand with me. Not someone who's going to run or close themselves off. Someone who will trust that together we can survive anything and that being apart exposes our greatest weaknesses."

"I want to be that someone. I'm sorry I couldn't be before." Bryant did extend his hand this time, and was shocked when Vaughn met him halfway. Not in a handshake, but by locking their fingers together. It was a simple gesture. Oddly intimate.

They stood there holding hands for a few moments before he continued. The heat and strength of Vaughn's hand, laced with his, and their palms pressed together, gave him the courage to put it all out there. "I'm never going to take you for granted or leave you to fend for yourself while I stuff my head up my ass again. And I think I might know a way to prove it."

"That's not what I'm asking for. This isn't one of your school tests for you to pass or fail." Vaughn shook his head. "I just need you to understand how I feel if we're going to find a way to fix this."

"I know, but I'm willing to do it anyway. I want you to tattoo me." Bryant took his phone out of his pocket with his free hand and pulled up the photos Vaughn had taken of him covered in ink. "Like this."

Vaughn's eyes widened. "But…"

Bryant interrupted, "I've thought a lot about this. It's what I want. I want to be the me I could be if I quit being afraid and go after what I want. The me that you see when no one else ever has."

"Damn," Vaughn whispered. "I honestly didn't think you were ever going to get to this place. Not after last time, at Sterling's—"

"I'm slow. But I'm here now. Will you do this?" Bryant hoped Vaughn knew this was about a hell of a lot more than a tattoo. But just in case… "Wait. Don't answer that yet. First, tell me what should have been in this gap, what was in that smudgy bit in the center of the actual drawing."

Vaughn shrugged. "Nothing. I never finished that part."

"Bullshit. You drew something and erased it." Bryant wouldn't cut him any slack. If he wanted the bold and confident Bryant, he was going to get it. He took the drawing from where he'd rolled it up and stuck it in his back pocket, comparing it side by side with the version Vaughn had drawn directly on his skin. He'd been staring at them like that when he'd first discovered the differences between the two.

"Fine. Fuck. It was my name." Vaughn's cheeks flamed. Even his neck turned red. Bryant couldn't ever remember him being bashful before. His heart skipped a beat as he realized he had just as much power over Vaughn as the other guy had over him. "It was foolish and egotistical, so I removed it."

"Put it back."

"What?"

"You heard me. Put. It. Back." Bryant shook the paper in Vaughn's direction. "I want it. Right there, where you originally had it."

"You *really* don't have to do that." Vaughn tried to break free, but Bryant kept hold of him. "I'm just glad you're home. Here. Where you belong."

Bryant insisted, "That may be. But I'm going to anyway. Because that's what *I* want. You. Not only on my skin, but also in my life. For as long as I'm alive. You're already taking up a lot of room in my heart and soul, so it seems only fair. If you won't do it, I'll find someone else who—"

"Bryant?" Vaughn jumped in.

"Yeah?"

"I'm the only man who will ever mark you, got that?" Vaughn asked, his old self snapping back in an instant.

Bryant smiled. "Yes, sir."

"Good. Now stop talking and get your ass downstairs or we're not going to make it out of here for a long fucking time." He put his hands on Bryant's shoulders and spun him around before giving him a tiny shove. "Because I am about to kiss the shit out of you and we both know it won't stop there."

"Maybe I'm okay with that." Bryant looked over his shoulder, ready to abandon Plan A for a much sexier Plan B, where they had make-up sex first and did the tattoo thing afterward.

"There will be plenty of time for that later," Vaughn promised. "Besides, did you know that tattooing turns me on?"

"I did notice you were ready to go every night after your shift, yeah." Bryant nodded and looked away again. "I just thought that was because I was up here in your bed waiting for you to finish working, though."

Vaughn fisted the back of Bryant's shirt and drew him up

short. He held Bryant in place as he jogged around to stand in front of him on the stairs. "You and tattooing both turn me on. It was a double whammy. Even more tired than I've ever been before, I couldn't wait to be inside you. It's been lonely these past few months. I've never had a dry spell this long in my life."

Secretly, Bryant was thrilled to hear that Vaughn had been sleeping alone. He wouldn't have blamed the guy if he'd found comfort elsewhere since they'd split, but it gave him a funny feeling in the pit of his stomach to think that maybe...just maybe...Vaughn had missed him as much as he'd missed Vaughn.

As if to make sure Bryant understood, Vaughn sealed their mouths. He caressed Bryant's lips with his own, sweeping them back and forth before settling in for a long, slow exchange. He seduced, and reassured, with gentle laps of his tongue and a steady pressure. They might have caved and gotten naked right there on the back steps if someone hadn't interrupted their make-up kiss.

A whistle cut through the air before a man shouted, "Hey, get a room!"

Vaughn's head whipped around as if he was prepared to kick ass if anyone so much as thought about insulting Bryant or their relationship. Until he realized it was Viho, who gave them a salute and a huge grin before dragging Sterling to their car, which had been parked in the lot behind the shops. She blew them a kiss before she climbed behind the wheel.

Well, at least his cousins would know he was going for it, taking their advice. And even if things went to shit—though he was pretty sure now that they wouldn't—they'd be there to pick him up.

Vaughn brushed the pad of his thumb over Bryant's lower lip. "You're even more delicious than I remembered. I never want to go so long without tasting you again."

Bryant gulped, then nodded. "Good idea."

"Let's go." Vaughn took his hand once more and led him through the back door of Cowboy Ink.

Bryant had waited until Vaughn's day off so they'd have the place to themselves if everything went according to his plan. It took Vaughn a little while to set his station up including wrapping everything in plastic, pouring ink from larger bottles into disposable cups, and whatever else he needed to do. Bryant didn't care. He got to stand there and watch his man work. Just being together, and not fighting, knowing they had all the time they wanted, was enough for the moment.

Vaughn sat on his swivel stool, then picked up his tattoo gun. He looked at Bryant then set it down again.

"What's wrong?" Bryant asked.

"You really trust me to mark you permanently?" Vaughn stared into his eyes as Bryant took a step closer, then another and another until they were less than a foot apart. "I don't want you to think you made another bad decision. This is forever. Be sure."

Bryant tipped Vaughn's face up. "Do you regret yours?"

"Whether or not you love me back, you'll always have this spot in my heart." Vaughn sighed. "But what's right for me might not be right for you."

"It is. You were always the right choice. You always will be."

Vaughn smiled. "Okay. Then take your shirt off and lay your sexy self down on my table."

"Oh, that sounds dirty." Bryant adjusted his hard-on as he settled in.

He'd watched Vaughn work enough nights that he knew what was coming next. Still, he had to bite his cheek to keep from groaning as Vaughn took extra care cleaning his chest and shaving it. That barest bit of contact was enough to make him wish they were up to something else right then.

He figured he'd have some time to cool off as Vaughn prepared a stencil for whatever he was about to do. Except just then Vaughn asked, "Do you trust me enough to do this freehand?"

"I trust you completely." Bryant blinked up at Vaughn, never more sure of anything in his life than that. "Do anything you want to me. I'm yours."

Vaughn seemed to relax then. He perched on his low stool and rolled closer, his face as intense as Bryant's had been when he'd occupied his own similar seat in his old laboratory.

The gun buzzed as Vaughn dunked the needles in the ink again. "No more joking around. This is serious business. Especially when I'm tattooing you, because I'm going to have to stare at this linework every time we make love for the rest of our lives."

"That was so romant—" Bryant started to melt until the first pass sank into his flesh. "Son of a bitch! A little warning would be nice."

"Shhh, Bryant. I'm working on my masterpiece."

He didn't say anything after that, but even hours of pain couldn't wipe the smile off his face.

17

They were making out before Bryant even saw the finished product. When Vaughn wiped him down, washing away the ink and blood with green soap, Vaughn's dick made him painfully aware of how long he'd been hard.

Hours.

Hell, months.

When Bryant had been gone, no one else would do. He wasn't like other guys, and that's exactly why Vaughn loved him so damn much. He was quiet. Nerdy and reserved. An all-around good person who would go out of his way to help anyone in need...even a stranger.

Sure, he liked to fuck, but he never once had made Vaughn feel as if that was the only reason they were together. He'd waited forever, and chosen Vaughn—only Vaughn—to share that intimacy with.

How could he not want to keep it that way?

Vaughn had tried to hook up again after Bryant. A few weeks after that disaster in Sterling's cottage, he'd picked up his old dating app and browsed through the flood of private messages he'd accumulated. Funny enough, he couldn't remember the last time he'd gone on there before then.

Not one of the many lascivious offers had appealed to him, though.

He'd deleted the thing off his phone entirely.

Bryant had changed him, just as permanently as Vaughn had just marked the other man. Hook-ups weren't good enough anymore, not when he knew what it was like to make love to someone he cared about. Someone he admired, and vowed to protect.

Someone he loved.

There. He'd admitted it, to himself at least.

Vaughn tore his mouth from Bryant's long enough to pocket a bottle of the coconut oil some of his clients preferred for aftercare, then grab Bryant's hand. He dragged the guy toward his office. "We can't fuck in the shop, but I'm not going to make it upstairs. My office. Now."

"On your desk?" Bryant asked, sounding more turned on than scandalized.

"No better way to make paying bills more fun. Now every time I'm working, I'll think of you. Of this night." Vaughn pressed Bryant against the wall, wincing slightly when his boyfriend's shoulders hit the surface harder than he'd intended. It was going to be nearly impossible to control himself. But he had to. The last thing he wanted was to frighten Bryant.

He was shocked when, instead of cringing, Bryant moaned.

"You like that?"

"Yeah." He nodded.

"You're not afraid?" He leaned in closer, careful to avoid putting too much pressure on Bryant's abraded skin.

"Never with you." He smiled that shy, lopsided smile Vaughn adored and said, "In fact, I kind of liked it. I want to be...more adventurous. Is that okay?"

It was the best compliment Vaughn had ever been given. One he swore he would always make sure he deserved. "Hell yes. Explore away."

"In that case..." Bryant eyed him as if he were one of those world-renowned Compass Ranch steaks and he hadn't eaten in months. "I was wondering—"

"What?" Vaughn ran his hands down Bryant's abdomen, toward his cock, which had nearly poked a hole in his jeans by then.

"Can I try fucking you?" Bryant's cheeks grew red, but he didn't look away.

Vaughn blinked up at Bryant. It wasn't very often that he was stunned like that.

"Never mind. I certainly would never force someone to do something they aren't into. What we've shared already was so much more than I hoped for. I can be happy with that. Ecstatic, really. If it's not your thing..."

Vaughn shifted, spinning so that his back was to the wall and Bryant loomed over him. "It hasn't been my thing before, but with you...who knows? Yeah, of course you can. Just...take it easy on me. It's probably been seven or eight years since I let someone do me."

Bryant growled low in his throat as he dipped his head and recaptured Vaughn's mouth. This time he took control, plunging his tongue into Vaughn's mouth as he pressed one thigh between Vaughn's. He was a natural. An even partner for Vaughn, just like he'd always known Bryant would be.

Fuck yes. This was what he'd been waiting for.

Vaughn gave himself over to the moment, letting Bryant undress himself before getting rid of Vaughn's clothes. He tried to stand still when Bryant rained kisses all over his body and toyed with his cock, bringing him nearly to the edge of coming before licking his lips and backing off.

"Should I make you come before I fuck you?" he asked.

"Nah, I'd rather be horny when you do," Vaughn said. "You and that big cock of yours are going to be a challenge, but I'm up for it."

Bryant nodded. "I'll take care of you. I swear."

Vaughn smiled and kissed Bryant lightly. "I know you will."

Then everything changed. Bryant's eyes turned stormy. He put his hand on Vaughn's lower back and ushered him to his desk. With a solid shove between his shoulder blades, Bryant bent Vaughn in half over his own desk and cupped the cheeks of his ass in his palm.

He squeezed them, massaged them, then finally spread them.

Vaughn's forehead pressed to the pile of paperwork he hadn't felt like finishing yesterday, wondering how he'd gotten here and how his entire life had changed in a matter of hours. Then he groaned as Bryant's fingers reached down to cup his balls.

Vaughn disclosed the bottle of oil in his pocket to Bryant, and begged him to be generous with it. Which he was. He coated his hands and Vaughn's ass. Then both of their cocks and balls, too.

Soon they were slipping and sliding against each other, their bodies primed for what was about to happen. Vaughn's heart was ready, too.

Bryant rubbed Vaughn's hole, then pressed a single digit into his body to start. That alone was enough to make his cock tick. Precome dribbled from the head of his dick down the side of his desk. It didn't get any less intense when Bryant worked a second and third finger into him, pumping slowly as he stretched Vaughn's ass.

Vaughn closed his eyes and clung to his desk. The sensations coursing through him were overwhelming, making him lost to rapture. Bryant's fingers disappeared, but only for a moment. And then there was something else in their place. Something blunt, hot, and thick.

Bryant's cock.

"Fuck me!" he yelled, needing to be joined once more with this man. It had been far too long that they'd been apart.

The strangled groan Bryant made as he sank into Vaughn's ass for the first time was all the reward Vaughn needed. Until he realized the pain he'd anticipated never materialized. And neither did the tension in his body that kept him from enjoying the act. With Bryant in charge of their love making, he learned just how good it could feel to have a man spreading him, invading the most private parts of him, sliding inside. "Ah, fuck. Bryant."

"Am I hurting you?" Bryant panted as he paused.

"No. Son of a bitch, don't quit now." Vaughn reached behind him, hooking his palm around the back of Bryant's thigh and using his grip to draw the other man closer.

Bryant started slow and careful before working up to a steady pace. He alternated long, deep strokes with short jabs that unerringly found Vaughn's prostate. Figured Bryant would be a natural. He'd probably studied Vaughn's technique subconsciously every time they'd fucked.

Vaughn's wonder grew as rapture built inside him, making him realize just how much he'd been missing out on by forsaking this pleasure. Then again, maybe it was only this fantastic because of who he was doing it with.

When Bryant had asked to fuck him, he'd been prepared to take it. To enjoy bringing Bryant pleasure and then to find his own after. Never had he thought it could be like this. That he could get off on being ridden when he never had before.

Another few strokes and—

"Bryant!" Vaughn cursed, wondering what the fuck had stopped the man right then. He lifted his head and saw their reflection in the mirrored window. Apparently just as Bryant himself had, too.

"Is that really us? I mean...me?" Bryant tipped his head, staring at the fierce, tattooed man who had his boyfriend pinned to his desk and was fucking the shit out of him in his workplace.

"Hell yes, it is." Vaughn rocked backward, encouraging Bryant to start moving again. He did, but with more control this time, a fluid grace neither of them had known he possessed. Damn, it felt good. Incredible, really. "Look at you. See what I see. Have always seen."

"I'm him." Bryant roared, then clasped his hands around Vaughn's waist. He anchored Vaughn as he began to fuck harder, deeper. Vaughn groaned when his balls swung below him, tapping the side of his desk. His cock was pointed downward against the cool metal. That didn't keep him from being every bit as hard as steel, though.

He shuffled backward just enough to jam his hand between the desk and his thighs, then fisted his cock. "Shit, yes. Fuck me. Bryant."

"Jerk your cock for me, Vaughn," Bryant snarled in his ear. "Show me how much you like this side of me. A side that's only for you. Always for you."

Son of a bitch. The guy was going to give him a heart attack. Vaughn rubbed himself faster, squeezing harder, and still it wasn't enough. The pressure of Bryant's growing cock inside him, caressing him from within, and the storm of passion raging around them couldn't last forever.

And still, Bryant fucked.

Vaughn tried his best to keep up, but after a while all he could do was cling to the desk with one hand and try to grant himself some relief with the other. When Bryant finally stiffened behind him, rammed deep, then held still, Vaughn knew this was it. Bryant was about to flood his ass with hot, silky come.

He was about to unleash himself inside a man for the first time, and he'd chosen Vaughn to give it to. The thought alone was enough to push him over the edge.

He fucked into his fist as his balls pulled up tight to his core. While Bryant tipped over the line from anticipation to detonation, Vaughn shot his own load onto the floor between their feet in time to his boyfriend's orgasmic spasms.

They climaxed simultaneously.

Shouted their euphoria to each other as they did it.

Vaughn's ass clenched around Bryant, drawing out his lover's pleasure. And knowing the other man was loving every moment of his release only enhanced Vaughn's ecstasy. He came until he was sure he'd die of dehydration.

Bryant sagged, resting on Vaughn's back as he kissed Vaughn's neck and ran his fingers over Vaughn's scalp. They were sweaty, exhausted, and so damn relieved to have found each other again that Vaughn almost didn't want to move.

Until he remembered that Bryant's tattoo wasn't even bandaged yet.

Bryant's dick slipped from his ass as Vaughn pushed straight once more. His legs trembled as he cleaned first Bryant, making sure to sanitize and cover his skin properly, and then himself before locking up the shop. They were quiet—content to share a hushed intimacy—until they climbed into bed, legs scissored and arms wrapped around each other.

"I'm so glad you're back." Vaughn whispered into the darkness, glad Bryant couldn't see the extra shine in his eyes.

"I'm so glad you'll have me." Bryant hugged him tight.

They fell asleep entwined with each other, and Vaughn was committed to making sure they never spent another night apart.

18

Bryant couldn't believe how much this mattered to Vaughn. It seemed like a simple thing, strolling down the street together holding hands. For them, it was huge.

It was important that his boyfriend realize he was glad to be seen together with him.

And secretly, Bryant suspected Vaughn liked to parade him around and make sure everyone knew who he belonged to. Bryant had never been the kind of person anyone wanted to show off before, but he was willing to admit he liked the feeling.

They talked about everything and nothing as they spent Vaughn's day off wandering around the downtown area of Laramie, Wyoming, one of the closest cities to Compton Pass. Sure, it wasn't a megalopolis like New York or L.A., but it was bigger and busier than their sleepy little town.

They walked along the main street, browsing through shop windows. It was incredible to spend time like this, like a normal couple. Bryant was hardly paying attention to the goods in the stores until they passed a high-end antique dealer, which ordinarily wouldn't have been his thing.

Except something caught his eye.

He stopped in his tracks, jerking Vaughn to a halt. Then he practically dragged the guy inside and over to a display case where he leaned in for a better look.

"You like that watch?" Vaughn asked subtly, maybe hinting around for Christmas or birthday ideas. Not that either of them could afford the one he was studying with his photographic memory.

"Of course I do. I've admired it my whole life...when my dad was wearing it. It was JD's." Bryant clenched his fists. Had his dad sold it to help raise some of the cash for Bryant's experiment? Oh shit, that couldn't be it, could it?

"Hang on a second, maybe it's just one similar..." Vaughn's grim face spoke volumes.

"It's not. See the tiny ding on the band? It's from when I was eight or nine. Doug and I were goofing around on the back of one of the tractors. His jacket got caught on a tree and tugged him off. He was heading straight under the tire until my dad jammed his hand down and grabbed him before something awful could happen. But the watch took the brunt of the impact. My dad always said it saved him from breaking his wrist that day. Besides, it's engraved to JD from Vicki." Bryant bent over with his hands on his knees.

Vaughn caught the eye of the shopkeeper and raised his hand. "Hi, could I take a look at this?"

"It's a beaut, that one. A rare find. Solid gold. Handcrafted by a master watchmaker, too. They don't make them like that anymore." The guy nodded as he unlocked the case. He was careful as he handed it to Vaughn, who immediately flipped it over.

With my timeless love...Vicki

Bryant thought he might be sick. Doubly so when he

caught sight of all the zeroes on the price tag. A perpetual student with no job, he couldn't even dream of affording it. His only option was to accept that this was what it had cost his family to support him in an effort that hadn't succeeded.

Might never succeed.

It was going to rain eventually, but until it did, he wouldn't even know if all this had been worth it. And what if it hadn't been?

He felt that familiar urge to run tugging at his boots.

Until he looked over at Vaughn. The creases around his mouth and between his brows made it clear he was wondering how Bryant would react. Would this be the wedge that drove them apart forever?

Not if Bryant had anything to say about it.

This time he wised up and leaned on Vaughn instead of shoving him away. They thanked the shopkeeper and left a significant piece of his family's history behind when they went back to the truck, where he slid across the bench seat to rest his head on Vaughn's shoulder, defeated. "I don't have any way to make this right. The system and all my improvements have to actually work before I can make any money from them. What am I going to say to my family? What will I say to my dad?"

Ah, fuck.

"I don't know, Bryant. But we'll figure out something. Your dad believes in you. If he didn't, he would never have done this. Think of it this way—he's so sure that your technology will advance the farm and the improve life for everyone involved that he was willing to gamble that watch on it." Vaughn shook Bryant's shoulders. "He's willing to let the past go in order to make the future better. He has faith in you. And so do I."

In that moment, there was only one thing Bryant knew to be true. So he didn't try to repress it. "I love you, Vaughn."

"I love you, too." Vaughn kissed his temple. "I know it's tough to deal with now, but this is going to be okay."

Bryant sat there for a while, wrapped in his lover's arms.

After he felt steady again, he reached for his phone and called Doug.

"Hey, there's the cousin I was just thinking of!" Doug joked.

"Why?" Bryant was afraid to hope. "Do you have good news? What's the weather doing?"

Doug turned his phone around so that the video transmitted an image of his laptop screen and the weather forecast running on it. It was blotchy with red blobs. *Rain.* Heavy rain everywhere.

Bryant held his breath as he reminded himself it was only a simulator the storm-chasing crew used. "You think it's actually coming?"

"Yeah, but I thought that the last four times there was a low pressure system over this way, too." His cousin shrugged. "The weather this summer is more confusing than a woman."

"Or a guy." Vaughn rolled his eyes so Bryant smacked him in the gut with the back of his hand.

If this rain didn't come, not only would the herd suffer, but the money his father had sunk into the irrigation and water retention systems would keep them from being able to ship more hay in from a neighboring farm.

Bryant might have fucked them all.

"Calm down." Vaughn rubbed Bryant's thigh out of sight of his phone.

"Sit tight, cuz. This can't last forever," Doug said.

"But will we make it until it rains again?" Bryant was pretty sure his nerves were shot. He needed to go home and let Vaughn distract him before he had a nervous breakdown.

Doug tried to help. "I'll bet you my autographed World Finals Rodeo poster that it'll be raining before morning."

Unfortunately, Bryant won that bet.

19

———

A couple days later, Bryant was sitting at the table in Sterling's cottage with Vaughn. They'd stayed out here the past few nights in case, as was forecasted, it finally fucking rained.

Of course it hadn't.

So he paced the kitchen some more.

Vaughn reached out and grabbed his wrist, tugging him into his lap. He banded his arms around Bryant, refusing to allow him to stand up again. "I love you, Bryant. But if you don't sit your ass down, I'm going to have to bum some rope off your uncles and tie you up."

"I'm trying my absolute hardest." Bryant swore his insides were being eaten through from all the acid churning in his gut.

He couldn't sleep. He couldn't eat. Hell, he couldn't even fuck.

"Look at the sky. It's coming. I can feel it in my ankle." Vaughn grimaced as he rotated it.

"The one you broke in eighth grade?" Bryant had nearly forgotten the summer Vaughn had been hobbling around on

175

crutches or the time he'd accepted a ride across the farm on Bryant's horse.

"It was worth it for that horseback ride you gave me over to my dad's place." Vaughn smiled as he hugged Bryant like he had back then.

"Once a perv, always a perv," Bryant teased.

"There's my boyfriend." Vaughn laughed. "I missed you. Stay here with me for a while. I think today's the day."

"Well, you should know." Bryant turned and kissed Vaughn gently. "After all, you broke *my* drought."

"I guess I did, didn't I?" Vaughn leaned in, about to make the sweltering kitchen even hotter when a bolt of blue-white light illuminated the sky an instant before the loudest clap of thunder Bryant had ever heard rattled the windows of his sister's house. There was no mistaking it this time. *Thunder!*

He looked over at Vaughn and grinned. Instead of shutting the blinds and standing back from the window like any sane weatherman would recommend for their safety, Bryant grabbed his boyfriend's hand and tugged.

"Where are you taking me?" Vaughn chuckled as he shook his head.

"Outside!" Bryant didn't waste any time. He bolted for the front door and flung it open. Wind whipped through the grass outside, birds dove for cover in the crispy leaves of the trees, and they ran out into the yard.

"You're going to get us killed, you lunatic!" Vaughn cringed when another series of flashes pinged around them.

Bryant didn't care. He stared up at the sky and the clouds rolling past overhead, hoping. For rain. For the rest of his prayers to be answered. "Come on. *Jake, please, help us out.*"

As if in answer, a big fat drop of rain fell and splattered right in his eye.

Bryant whooped and swiped it away as he turned to Vaughn. "It's raining!"

"Yes, yes, it is." He held his arms out, palms up, and collected the moisture that began to splash down in more and more spots around them. "You think Jake heard you?" Vaughn whispered.

"I'm not sure, but if so... I hope he looks away now." Bryant started to strip. He wasn't wasting this chance to celebrate with the love of his life. Thankfully the cottage blocked the view between where they were standing and Sterling and Viho's house.

"What the hell are you doing?" Vaughn stared at him as if he'd lost his mind.

Bryant met his gaze and held it as he removed the rest of his clothes. For the first time in his life, he felt confident enough to seduce the man he wanted more than anything. Even more than the rain. "Remember that shower sex you wanted? How's rain sex sound instead?"

"A rain check. Nice. I'm in." Vaughn kicked off his boots and practically ripped his shirt in half as he yanked it from his jeans. Periodic bursts of light outlined his six-pack, which was growing wetter by the second.

The patter and plop of moisture turned into a constant barrage. Then they were soaked.

So much water fell from the sky that Bryant couldn't even hear himself as he called out to Vaughn. It didn't matter. The other guy responded as if he knew what Bryant needed. Maybe even needed it himself.

They came together in the wide-open yard behind the cottage. Damn anyone else who might happen by. A stream of warm water poured from Bryant's hair and down his face. His chest slapped against Vaughn's when they collided with enough momentum to make him wonder if the thunder was coming from within him.

The effect Vaughn had on him was powerful enough to be its own force of nature.

For a moment or two they stood there, peering into each other's eyes. Crystalline drops beaded on Vaughn's onyx lashes, making them glisten.

Then he closed the gap between them, crushing his mouth to Bryant's.

Their groans smashed together like the warm and cold fronts above them, mingling and turning into the perfect storm of passion. Bryant sank to his knees at Vaughn's feet, craving the taste of him. He filled his mouth with heat and cock, sucking just the way his partner preferred.

The clench of Vaughn's hands on Bryant's shoulders guaranteed he was having the effect he intended. But it wasn't long before they both needed more. He pulled off and began to lie back.

"No, you're not going to lay in the dirt while I fuck you." Vaughn kept him from settling into the muddy area forming around them.

He turned and splayed himself on the ground instead, then held his arms out to Bryant, whose heart ka-thumped a little at the tender side his gruff boyfriend sometimes unwittingly showed.

Bryant followed Vaughn's urging and crouched over his torso. Vaughn locked his hands onto Bryant's quads, then guided him upward until his cock dangled near Vaughn's mouth.

His boyfriend lunged upward, taking the shaft between his lips and sucking. He didn't screw around, instead applying just the right amount of suction to border on discomfort while pumping up Bryant's cock as rapidly as possible.

Meanwhile, he reached beneath Bryant. The hum that radiated along Bryant's shaft made him fairly certain the other guy had taken his own cock in hand and started to jerk himself off. Thank God, because he wanted Vaughn inside him, as deep as he could go, while they enjoyed the storm raging around—and within—them.

"I need you to fuck me, Vaughn. Now. Please." Begging didn't bother him in the least. Vaughn wouldn't lord his needs over him.

"Wait, Bryant. Lube." Vaughn grunted as he tried to prevent Bryant from descending, putting his ass in prime range for fucking. "Damn it. I don't want to hurt you."

Vaughn's head sank onto the dampening ground.

"It's a good thing I was wearing this then, huh?" Bryant grinned as he took Vaughn's hand and brought it to his ass. He gasped when his boyfriend nudged the base of the generously lubed plug he'd had in all day in the hopes that Vaughn would take him for a hard ride later, either because it'd finally be raining and they were celebrating like they were now, or because he needed to be soothed after more disappointment.

It looked like all his wishes were coming true today.

"You're a fucking genius, has anyone ever told you that?" Vaughn grinned as he teased the toy from Bryant's body and chucked it into a flowerbed nearby.

They had, but it had never meant as much to Bryant as it did right then. Knowing he made his boyfriend happy was damn near as enjoyable as the pressure of Vaughn's cock nudging his ass, seeking entry.

Bryant watched rain splash onto Vaughn's abs, saw them clenching beneath the sheen of the fresh, clean water pouring over them. He shook his head to clear some of the moisture from his eyes so that he could see the expression on Vaughn's face when they were joined once again.

Even though it had only been half a day since they'd been linked like this, their connection had the power to electrify him. He sank onto Vaughn's cock, bit by bit, working himself down as his boyfriend thrust upward.

Together, they made themselves fit each other. If there was

a tiny bit of residual pain, Bryant didn't mind. He knew that they'd get past it and give each other far more pleasure than that initial pinprick of discomfort.

He sighed when Vaughn's thighs cradled his lower back and his balls rested against Vaughn's belly.

"Don't get too comfortable there, Doc." Vaughn laughed as he reached down to run a finger along the entire length of Bryant's cock. "You've got some riding to do."

One of Vaughn's palms connected with the side of Bryant's ass, then gripped it, using the hold to help him get started. His other hand concentrated on massaging Bryant's cock and balls, which were presented for him to easily play with. Their position also let Vaughn openly admire the artwork Bryant wore with honor.

It was nearly complete now, after more sessions than he could count. Someday soon he'd show his cousins and his father and uncles. He finally felt like a fully fledged Compton, wearing symbols of their ranch, their ancestors, his profession, and—of course—Vaughn's name.

The calluses on Vaughn's hands, at the base of his fingers, only added to the rough edge of his steady grip. He pumped Bryant in time to the rhythm Bryant set as he began to fuck himself on Vaughn's cock. Bryant put his hands behind him and braced them on Vaughn's knees, using the leverage to help him pick up speed.

His hips rose and fell, working Vaughn's cock in and out of himself. Watching the heavy-lidded stare Vaughn gave him as they fucked had his own dick jerking in his boyfriend's grip.

"Fuck yes, Bryant," Vaughn cheered into the storm. "Ride me. Show me how much you love this. Come all over me and I'll fill you up."

How could Bryant resist a dirty-talking not-cowboy like that?

He stared straight into Vaughn's eyes as he surrendered to

the moment. He embraced the rapture streaking through him as bright as the lightning striking around them, adding drops of his own fluid to the rain spattering all over Vaughn's torso. Vaughn angled his chin down and lapped a pearly line from his own pectoral muscle, sampling the proof of Bryant's pleasure.

And then his cock bulged inside Bryant's ass a moment before he began to buck.

True to his word, Vaughn deposited jet after jet inside Bryant, his fists pounding the ground, sending water spraying in every direction. Though the wind shrieked and the storm seethed, all Bryant heard was that guttural gasp of ecstasy that he'd inspired.

Then he collapsed beside Vaughn.

They lay there, staring up at the sky, being washed clean of all their fear, doubts, and worry. Until, after a while, the summer rain brought chills to even the toasty places where they connected.

"You're dying to go check the system, aren't you?" Vaughn asked.

"Yeah. Do you mind?" Bryant bit his lip.

Vaughn climbed to his feet, then held his hand out for Bryant. "Not at all. How can I help?"

Bryant ran for the cottage. "Just stay with me while I do my thing and don't let me freak out if things aren't as they should be."

"That's not a problem, but we should probably rinse off and get dressed first."

"Good thinking."

Vaughn was never more than a step behind as they splashed through puddles, inspected connections, and monitored the water levels while the retention ponds began to fill. Everything worked perfectly.

Hours later, Bryant felt solid enough to return to the cottage. Once there, Vaughn grabbed a blanket off the back of the couch and wrapped it around them both, bundling them together.

They stood, dripping and shivering, in the entryway, hugging each other and slow dancing in place until the chill began to fade from his fingers and toes. It would be impossible not to be warm in Vaughn's arms.

"Rainy days are my new favorite," Vaughn purred.

"Mine too." Bryant squeezed him tight enough he might be smothering the other guy. Still, he refused to let go. "Though with you, any day is amazing."

"But especially the wet ones."

Bryant laughed and nodded. "Especially those."

"Even though you're a stubborn-ass Compton, I love you, Bryant. I think I have from the first moment I saw you. I don't ever want to lose you again." Vaughn took Bryant's palm. He smoothed it over his heart and the tattoo he wore so proudly there. "I'll do my best to make sure you're never hurt again, especially because of me."

"I've told you a million times. That wasn't your fault. None of this was your—"

"And it sure as fuck wasn't yours either." Vaughn shook his head. "But it screwed us both up anyway. No more. That's done and so is the running. If there's trouble, we'll deal with it together and come out stronger for it."

"Deal." Bryant choked when Vaughn loosened the blanket just enough to drop to one knee.

"I never imagined doing this buck-ass naked, but what the fuck? You see all of me, loved all of me when no one else thought I was worth it."

"You do the same for me," Bryant whispered, his voice somewhere down around his ankles.

"So...will you be my partner for life? Marry me?" Vaughn asked.

Bryant swallowed hard so that he could roar. "Hell yes!"

He put his hands beneath Vaughn's arms and lifted him up, like they'd always do for each other. "But..."

"No. No buts allowed. It's a yes or no question." Vaughn bit his lip as if he had any reason at all to worry.

"I'm just wondering... I know you asked me, but I'd love it if you would become a Compton." It was a dumb detail. His mind specialized in facts, though, and now that he'd thought of it, he couldn't imagine it any other way.

"You think your family would want me having their name?" Vaughn asked.

Considering how serious he was when he said it, Bryant knew without a doubt he would insist the other guy take it. Convince him he was as worthy of it as any of the rest of them. "Of course they would be proud to give it to you. Snake was an honorary Compton. It feels right that you should make it official."

"I would love that." Vaughn hugged him tight. "Nearly as much as I love you."

Of course, that led to more kissing, and more fucking—this time the long and slow variety in the comfort of their bed. The entire time, it rained. And rained. And rained. Until Compass Ranch's water retention system overflowed, filled to the brim like Bryant's heart and soul.

20

———

TWO MONTHS LATER

"The results are in." Bryant raced outside to the informal Sunday gathering the Compass Boys, their sisters, and their parents had started having now that the weather had cooled off some. He held up a thick sheaf of papers. "After eight weeks of operation at full capacity, we've used seventy-two percent less water than our baseline and have been able to reclaim enough of that to fully restock the storage systems, even with less than two inches of precipitation during that time."

"That's amazing, son." Sam slapped him on the shoulder. "I could tell by our bills that we were consuming a hell of a lot less. But...what about your degree?"

"It's official. After seeing these reports, the board unanimously approved my project. Dr. Burgess will personally be hooding me at the winter commencement ceremony. They also submitted my data to an award panel for innovation in agriculture, and they think it's likely that I could win. The prize is a hundred thousand dollars toward implementation of the ideas in the paper. So...I could pay you back, Dad."

"You've already given the ranch its money's worth." Sam

smiled. "Use anything that comes of this to start your own business. One where you can install this stuff at other farms. No reason you can't do good and prosper, too."

Bryant nodded. He wanted to argue, because he knew how much his family had sacrificed to push him ahead and it still wasn't sitting right with him. He'd told Vaughn how he felt and they'd been working through it together. As a team. He still hadn't figured out the right solution, but together they would eventually.

As if Vaughn could read his mind, he pulled Bryant aside. "I think this would be a good time to give this back to your dad."

He pressed something cool and heavy into Bryant's hand. When Bryant got a good look at it, he nearly choked. "JD's watch? How? Hang on, is this why you sold your truck?"

"Like I said, we pretty much go everywhere together. We don't need two vehicles right now. This was more important to you and your family. For us." Vaughn smiled softly. "I would have told you sooner, but it wasn't a done deal until this morning, while you were giving your presentation to the board. I went back to the shop with the sales money last week but the watch was gone. I had to track it down again and make a deal with the new owner. I didn't want to get your hopes up until I knew I could pull it off. Anyway, I won't let you lose something this important if there's anything I can do about it. Not now or ever."

If Bryant hadn't already been madly in love with Vaughn, he would have fallen right then. But like his father, who'd obviously traded a material possession for the good of his family, Bryant needed Vaughn to understand that what they shared was priceless. "I couldn't have done any of this without you. No matter what the outcome had been today, I was at peace with it, because I knew that I'd walk out here after that videoconference, and you'd be waiting for me."

"That's true. I have your back. I always will." He closed Bryant's hand around the watch. "And that's why I did this."

Bryant flew to Vaughn and crushed him in a bear hug that the guy returned after a moment or two. Right there on the ranch, surrounded by everyone who meant anything to him, Bryant no longer gave a fuck who saw. In fact, he was proud to be Vaughn's man.

"I'm so happy for you two," Bryant's mom Cindi murmured from nearby. "I never wanted anything except for you kids to be as happy as your father and I have been for so long. I can't wait for your wedding and for Vaughn to be my son-in-law on paper, like he already is in my heart."

"It means a lot to me to be part of your family. It's something I've always wanted, and never had." Vaughn cleared his throat.

Cindi nodded, unable to speak. Was she knuckling away a tear? Oh God, Bryant couldn't survive his mom crying, especially since he could count the number of times he'd seen her do it on one hand. To distract her, he turned to her and his father, who—as always—was right by her side.

Bryant lifted the watch, carefully cradled in his palm, and held it out to them. "I think this belongs to you."

If he thought returning the heirloom to his father would stem his mom's tears, he miscalculated. Because they escalated into sobbing. "Is that—? How?"

Sam staggered back a step. The commotion began to draw the attention of the rest of the family. Bryant's uncles Silas, Seth, and Sawyer huddled around his dad, making sure he was okay.

When Uncle Silas saw the watch, he cursed.

Even Uncle Sawyer took off his hat and stared.

Uncle Seth cleared his throat and said, "I guess what they say is true. What's meant to be..."

Bryant didn't waver. He clutched Vaughn's hand and said,

"Thank you for believing in me and for all the sacrifices you made for us, even when you didn't let us know there was a price to be paid."

"It looks like it was all worth it. You kids are turning out pretty damn fine. JD and Vicki...and Jake...would be even more proud than we are," Sam said, and his brothers nodded in agreement.

Bryant was in danger of joining his mom then, so he turned toward his cousins with Vaughn still holding his hand tight. If he spied Austin blinking rapidly or James staring at Ivy, he couldn't blame them either.

Doug, however, knew just what to do to save them from an emotional free-for-all. He grimaced. "Hey guys, somebody missing this?"

He tossed something stubby and black at Vaughn, who snatched it out of midair and jammed it into the pocket of his jeans before any of the older—or younger—generation could see what it was. The rest of the Compass Boys, however, started cracking up. Austin, Hayden, James, Ivy, and Doug drew attention away from the sentimental moment with their riot of hoots and snorts.

"What—?" Bryant started to ask Vaughn before he remembered the night they had fucked in the rain. Right about where Doug had planted his lawn chair. Oops.

Vaughn grinned as he put an arm around Bryant's shoulders and whispered in his ear, "Don't worry. He's just jealous he doesn't have wild sex with that girl of his out in the storms they chase."

Doug grimaced, but said, "I'm happy for you, Bryant. We all are. For finishing school and for finding someone to spend the rest of your life with. I never figured I'd be the last one of us to hold down the bachelor fort considering my wicked good looks and irresistible charm."

"For the record, I found Vaughn a long time ago. It just took forever to work things out." Bryant leaned closer to his partner, grateful that they were finally together and would never break apart again. "That could be the same for you."

"I'm not that patient." Doug shrugged, then drained his beer before reaching for another from the old metal washtub filled with ice. Bryant let it go. For now.

Sterling came outside then, carrying something heavy. Viho rushed to her side and took a fancy cake covered in blue icing that looked like waves from her, carrying it over to the table and adding it to the mountain of food his relatives had brought with them.

"What were you all going to do if I failed?" Bryant wondered.

"Celebrate your other successes and help you drown your misery in beer and cake. What else is family for?" Sterling grinned as she patted his cheek.

Lomasi wedged herself between them and said, "Or we could have just scraped the icing off and ate it when you weren't around like we did last time, Uncle Bryant."

Her parents looked horrified enough that he knew she was telling the truth. Vaughn squeezed him, as if trying to shelter him from the memories. He didn't need to, though Bryant loved the heat and weight of him nearby, as he would always be from then on.

He laughed and laughed. Something that had hurt him so much no longer had the power to do so. He was finally ready to let go of all the mistakes he'd made in the past and fully embrace his future.

As often as he'd prayed for rain, he was now looking forward to basking in years of sunny times.

Just like these.

WHAT HAPPENS NEXT?

If you've enjoyed Still Waters, be sure to check out the continuing Compass saga in Light As Air—Compass Boys Book Four—for Doug's story.

If you haven't already read the rest of the Compass saga, be sure to go back and read all about the original Compass brothers (Silas, Seth, Sam, and Sawyer) and their daughters, the Compass Girls (Sienna, Hope, Jade, and Sterling). The first three Compass Boys books (Austin, James, and Bryant) are also available now.

The adventure begins with Northern Exposure. Click here to find out more.

ABOUT THE AUTHORS

Jayne Rylon and Mari Carr met at a writing conference in June 2009 and instantly became arch enemies. Two authors couldn't be more opposite. Mari, when free of her librarian-by-day alter ego, enjoys a drink or two or... more. Jayne, allergic to alcohol, lost huge sections her financial-analyst mind to an epic explosion resulting from Mari gloating about her hatred of math. To top it off, they both had works in progress with similar titles and their heroes shared a name. One of them would have to go.

The battle between them for dominance was a bloody, but short one, when they realized they'd be better off combining their forces for good (or smut). With the ink dry on the peace treaty, they emerged as good friends, who have a remarkable amount in common despite their differences, and their writing partnership has flourished. Except for the time Mari attempted to poison Jayne with a bottle of Patron. Accident or retaliation? You decide.

Join Mari's newsletter and Jayne's Naughty News so you don't miss new releases, contests, or exclusive subscriber-only content.

Find Jayne Rylon on the web:
Twitter - @JayneRylon
Facebook - JayneRylon

<u>www.jaynerylon.com</u>
contact@jaynerylon.com

Find Mari Carr on the web at

www.maricarr.com
mari@maricarr.com

ALSO BY JAYNE RYLON

MEN IN BLUE

Hot Cops Save Women In Danger

Night is Darkest

Razor's Edge

Mistress's Master

Spread Your Wings

Wounded Hearts

Bound For You

DIVEMASTERS

Sexy SCUBA Instructors By Day, Doms On A Mega-Yacht By Night

Going Down

Going Deep

Going Hard

POWERTOOLS

Five Guys Who Get It On With Each Other & One Girl. Enough Said?

Kate's Crew

Morgan's Surprise

Kayla's Gift

Devon's Pair

Nailed to the Wall

Hammer it Home

More the Merrier *NEW*

HOT RODS

Powertools Spin Off. Keep up with the Crew plus...

Seven Guys & One Girl. Enough Said?

King Cobra

Mustang Sally

Super Nova

Rebel on the Run

Swinger Style

Barracuda's Heart

Touch of Amber

Long Time Coming

STANDALONE

Menage

Middleman

4-Ever Theirs

Nice & Naughty

Contemporary

Where There's Smoke

Report For Booty

COMPASS BROTHERS

Modern Western Family Drama Plus Lots Of Steamy Sex

Northern Exposure

Southern Comfort

Eastern Ambitions

Western Ties

COMPASS GIRLS

Daughters Of The Compass Brothers Drive Their Dads Crazy And Fall In Love

Winter's Thaw

Hope Springs

Summer Fling

Falling Softly

COMPASS BOYS

Sons Of The Compass Brothers Fall In Love

Heaven on Earth

Into the Fire

Still Waters

Light as Air

PLAY DOCTOR

Naughty Sexual Psychology Experiments Anyone?

Dream Machine

Healing Touch

RED LIGHT

A Hooker Who Loves Her Job

Complete Red Light Series Boxset

FREE - Through My Window - FREE

Star

Can't Buy Love

Free For All

PICK YOUR PLEASURES

Choose Your Own Adventure Romances!

Pick Your Pleasure

Pick Your Pleasure 2

RACING FOR LOVE

MMF Menages With Race-Car Driver Heroes

Complete Series Boxset

Driven

Shifting Gears

PARANORMALS

Vampires, Witches, And A Man Trapped In A Painting

Paranormal Double Pack Boxset

Picture Perfect

Reborn

PENTHOUSE PLEASURES

Naughty Manhattanite Neighbors Find Kinky Love

Taboo

Kinky

Sinner

ALSO BY MARI CARR

Compass

Northern Exposure

Southern Comfort

Eastern Ambitions

Western Ties

Winter's Thaw

Hope Springs

Summer Fling

Falling Softly

Into the Fire

Heaven on Earth

Still Waters

Second Chances:

Fix You

Dare You

Just You

Near You

Reach You

Always You

Sparks in Texas:

Sparks Fly

Waiting for You

Something Sparked

Off Limits

No Other Way

Whiskey Eyes

Trinity Masters:

Elemental Pleasure

Primal Passion

Scorching Desire

Forbidden Legacy

Hidden Devotion

Elegant Seduction

Secret Scandal

Delicate Ties

Beloved Sacrifice

Masterful Truth

Masters' Admiralty

Treachery's Devotion

Wild Irish:

Come Monday

Ruby Tuesday

Waiting for Wednesday

Sweet Thursday

Friday I'm in Love

Saturday Night Special

Any Given Sunday

Wild Irish Christmas

Wild Irish Boxed Set

Wilder Irish:

January Girl

February Stars

Guardian Angel

March Wind

Big Easy:

Blank Canvas

Crash Point

Full Position

Rough Draft

Triple Beat

Winner Takes All

Going Too Fast

Boys of Fall:

Free Agent

Red Zone

Wild Card

Clandestine:

Bound by the Past

Covert Affairs

Scoring

Mad about Meg

Cocktales

Party Naked

Screwdriver

Bachelor's Bait

Screaming O

Cowboy Heat

Spitfire

Rekindled

Inflamed

Farpoint Creek

Outback Princess

Outback Cowboy

Outback Master

Outback Lovers

June Girls:

No Recourse

No Regrets

Just Because:

Because of You

Because You Love Me

Because It's True

Love Lessons

Slam Dunk

Happy Hour

Madison Girls

Kiss Me Kate

Three Reasons Why

Scoundrels

Black Jack

White Knight

Red Queen

What Women Want

Sugar and Spice

Everything Nice

What Women Want

Individual Titles:

Power Play

Rough Cut

Seducing the Boss

Tequila Truth

Erotic Research

One Daring Night

Assume the Positions

Do Over

Bundles

Cowboy Heat

What Women Want

Wild Irish Boxed Set

Trinity Masters Boxed Set: Volumes 1-4

WHAT WAS YOUR FAVORITE PART?

Did you enjoy this book? If so, please leave a review and tell your friends about it. Word of mouth and online reviews are immensely helpful and greatly appreciated.

JAYNE'S SHOP

Check out Jayne's online shop for autographed print books,
direct download ebooks, reading-themed apparel up to size
5XL, mugs, tote bags, notebooks, Mr. Rylon's wood (you'll have
to see it for yourself!) and more.
www.jaynerylon.com/shop

LISTEN UP!

The majority of Jayne's books are also available in audio format on Audible, Amazon and iTunes.